Singing
Songs

Meg Tilly

Singing Songs

A DUTTON BOOK

DUTTON

Published by the Penguin Group
Penguin Books USA Inc., 375 Hudson Street, New York, New York 10014, U.S.A.
Penguin Books Ltd, 27 Wrights Lane, London W8 5TZ, England
Penguin Books Australia Ltd, Ringwood, Victoria, Australia
Penguin Books Canada Ltd, 10 Alcorn Avenue, Toronto, Ontario, Canada M4V 3B2
Penguin Books (N.Z.) Ltd, 182–190 Wairau Road, Auckland 10, New Zealand

Penguin Books Ltd, Registered Offices:
Harmondsworth, Middlesex, England

First published by Dutton, an imprint of Dutton Signet,
a division of Penguin Books USA Inc.
Distributed in Canada by McClelland & Stewart Inc.

First Printing, June, 1994
10 9 8 7 6 5 4 3 2 1

REGISTERED TRADEMARK—MARCA REGISTRADA

LIBRARY OF CONGRESS CATALOGING IN PUBLICATION DATA
Tilly, Meg.
    Singing songs / by Meg Tilly.
      p. cm.
    ISBN 0-525-93778-1
    1. Sexually abused children—United States—Fiction.   2. Family—
United States—Fiction.   3. Girls—United States—Fiction.
I. Title.
PS3570.I434S57   1994
813'.54—dc20   93–43203
                                              CIP

Printed in the United States of America
Set in Caslon 540, Caslon Open Face and Mistral
Designed by Steven N. Stathakis

To my mother,
with deepest thanks
for her love,
support, and friendship

Singing

Songs

One

Mama's Important Visitor

When Susan, Matthew and Mama got home from school, Mama was in a real hurry. Just paid the baby-sitter and pushed her out the door. Then upstairs she raced, two steps at a time, taking off her schoolteacher clothes as she went.

"I'm hungry, Mama!" yelled Matthew up the stairs after her. "I'm real hungry!"

"Then make a peanut butter sandwich."

"I don't want a peanut butter sandwich! I don't like peanut butter!"

"Well, that's too bad! I'm too busy! I have a very important visitor coming by!" Then she came thundering back down the stairs in one of Daddy's old shirts and her pale blue slacks with stains on them.

I wish I had one of Daddy's old shirts. I wouldn't wear it to clean in. I'd wear it for real clothes every day. And at night too, for p.j.'s. But it's too late now. All of Daddy's old clothes are already Mama's cleanup clothes or ripped-up rags for scrubbing.

Anyway, Mama was wearing her cleanup clothes, and proceeded to scrub the apartment from top to bottom.

Matthew followed her from room to room.

"Mama, I'm hungry . . ." "I'm hungry, Mama . . ." "I'm real hungry!"

But Mama just ignored him, her mouth set in a small straight line, wisps of brown hair escaping from her school bun. Just ignored him and kept on cleaning. Cleaning and mopping and vacuuming. Everything!

Finally he gave up and went into the kitchen and made a peanut butter sandwich.

After she finished cleaning we went upstairs and sat on her bed and watched her get dressed. She peeled off her cleanup clothes and dashed to the bathroom. "Oh my god . . . oh my god," she moaned. "Look at the time." She put her foot up on the sink and washed her bottom.

"Why are you doing that, Mama?" asked Katie. Mama pretended not to hear her. But that never stopped Katie. *"Why are you doing that, Mama? Why are you washing your bottom?"*

"Because I'm a grown-up." Then she sniffed under her arms, and splashed some water under there too.

Mama tried on one outfit after another. Finally she

settled on a cream-colored peasant blouse and skirt. The blouse had puffy short sleeves and embroidered flowers and red trim. And a scooped neck that slipped off her shoulders, making her neck look even longer than usual.

The skirt, which was my favorite, had little Mexican men in big, big hats and Mexican ladies in colorful dresses holding hands all around the bottom.

Mama took her hair out of her bun and brushed it until it danced around her face and shoulders, clinging and snapping so much that if I had a balloon, and put it on her head, it would have stayed there for sure.

Then she powdered her nose, made goldfish lips and put on her red, red lipstick.

Off went the glasses and up she stood twirling around in front of the mirror. Squinting slightly, turning this way and that.

"You look so beautiful, Mama," said Susan, her voice coming out all breathy.

"Yeah!" said me and Katie. "You look beautiful, Mama!"

Mama made a puffing noise through her lips. "I've got gray hair." Then she smiled at the mirror and went over to the closet. It took a while for Mama to find her sandals on account of her not wearing her glasses. So I helped her.

As she was buckling them, the doorbell rang.

Her face flushed.

"Go get the door, Susan," fingers fumbling with the buckle.

"No. I look yucky."

Mama grabbed her glasses off the dresser and put them on.

"Oh my god!" she gasped. "What is that stuff all over you?"

"Mud!" Katie piped up. "We were making mud pies."

The doorbell rang again.

"Well quick! Run wash your faces and change your clothes!" They just stood there. *"Hop to it!"* bellowed Mama. So they did.

Then Mama turned her eye on me. "You look okay, Anna, run answer the door."

I stood there stuck, cotton in my mouth.

The doorbell rang again, followed by a knock.

"Go on," she said, giving me a nudge. "Answer the door."

"I can't, Mama . . . I can't . . ." My voice hard to find. *"Answer the door!"*

"I'm scared, Mama . . ." My voice climbing higher.

"Oh for crying out loud!" She grabbed my arm with one hand, the hairbrush in the other, and swiped at my hair on the way downstairs. She caught my ear with the brush and it hurt.

To the door we went, sandals flip flopping.

Hairbrush on the bookshelf, glasses in her pocket. Big breath, smile, and she swung open the door.

"Hello, Richard," she says, her voice all soft and smooth. And I hide behind her skirt. Her skirt with the Mexican ladies and men holding hands round and round and round.

"Hello, Jean," says a deep man's voice. There is a slight pause and then he says, "God you're beautiful."

And she laughs. A low-sounding laugh in the back of her throat.

I peek around her and I see him. Standing there. Tall, so tall. Gray hair, cut short, like a lawn mower ran over his head. The porch light shining down on him. After that, darkness.

"Hi there," he says, smiling. Smiling big. Lots of teeth. I start to cry.

"Say hello," says Mama, trying to make me let go of her skirt. "Say hello to Mr. Smith." But I just cry harder. Making wet marks on her cream-colored skirt.

"She's just shy," says Mama with red ears and a laugh.

Then she takes me into the bedroom. Her hand so tight on my arm, I think it will fall off. She shuts the door and shakes me and shakes me. Whispering through clenched teeth, "Stop it! Stop it! What are you trying to prove? What?"

But I can't answer cause she is shaking me too hard.

So I have to stay in the bedroom all night, cause I disgraced the family. And I listen to Susan, Katie and Matthew eating special treats. Eating special treats and laughing. Laughing with Mr. Smith and it sounds like they're having fun.

Mrs. Watson

Mama threw out the TV. Just yanked it out of the wall. The next day Susan took me and Katie out behind the apartment and there it was. All gray and lifeless, perched on the top of the garbage can.

"Look," Susan said solemnly. "Our TV."

"Why is our TV in the garbage?" asked Katie, cocking her head sideways like a little bird.

"Because it's bad, and Mama doesn't want us watching it anymore."

"But I like our TV."

I was shuffling my feet back and forth, trying to figure out my feelings.

"I want our TV back!" said Katie.

"I don't," and I kicked the garbage can. Kicked it hard. Hurt my toe but I didn't show it. "I'm glad it's gone. It gave me bad dreams."

I had been watching *Dark Shadows* when Mama came home. A man was turning into a werewolf. It was scary and I was crying. Didn't even notice Mama came home. Didn't notice her until she yanked the cord out of the wall and made the bad man go away.

"No TV! No TV! How many times do I have to tell you!"

"It wasn't me, ma'am," said Mrs. Watson, looking at Mama's bellybutton. "It wasn't me. Must of been those kids of yours, can't make 'em behave no matter what I do."

"I don't care *who* it was. When I leave you here you are in charge! It is up to you to make sure that the rules are upheld. And rule number one is no TV!"

"I'm sorry, ma'am, but it's not my fault."

It's funny how grown-ups lie, and yet they tell you not to.

Well that night I had bad dreams. Dreamt the werewolf man was coming after me. All hairy and long claws and teeth. I must have been screaming loud, cause I woke up Mama and she brought me into bed with her and I nestled up into her soft bosom, all safe and cozy and warm. And the next morning, no TV.

"Where's the TV?" said Mrs. Watson, looking around.

"Gone," says Mama standing there, arms folded across her chest. "The TV is gone." Then she kissed us and went to work.

Mrs. Watson was mad. Said it was all my fault. Now what was she going to do all day! Huh? What was she going to do! She started cleaning cupboards, and then she found Mama's liquor cabinet. She was thirsty. Real thirsty. Drank a lot and then fell asleep. One minute she's standing, muttering something about something, I'm not sure what. And the next minute, *crash!* She's fast asleep right smack dab in the middle of our living room floor.

She wouldn't wake up no matter what. We pulled up her eyelid to see if she was faking. But she wasn't. She just lay there and let us. Didn't whack us or anything. Just lay there, red eyeball rolling. So we pretended Mama's bed was a trampoline. It was fun.

Mrs. Watson slept for a long time. Didn't wake up

until Mama came home from work and poured a big pot of cold water on her head. And let me tell you it sure did the trick. She woke up with a big *squawk!* And then when she saw Mama she let out another one, like she'd seen a ghost or something.

So anyway Mama says she's not sure what she's gonna do, but for the time being, Katie and I get to go to school with her, even though Katie's three and I'm four and a half. And we get to sit in her classroom, and have a lunch and everything. I'm so excited!

The Wedding

Mr. Smith came over for dinner again. Put me on his knee and stroked my head with his big clammy hand. Told me he had a little girl my exact same age, and twins, Nick and Faith. "My little girl's name's Joy," he said. "Isn't that pretty?"

"When's her birthday?" I ask, trying to be polite.

"When is Joy's birthday . . . humm . . . good question." He starts laughing, and spanks Mama's bottom as she walks by. "Let me see, it's sometime in December if that's any help."

"Christmas?"

"No, not on Christmas. I'm not sure what day, but I'll give you the year, nineteen fifty-nine. How's that?"

Then Susan cuts in, "Then she's not the same age."

"Susan!" Mama says like she's done something wrong. "Stop nitpicking."

"But she's five, Mama, she's five and a half and Anna is only four and a half! She's closer to my age than Anna's!"

"That's enough!" says Mama, her mouth making a small thin line.

When Mama tucks me in that evening she asks me if I like him. I look in her face and can see that she wants me to lie, so I say yes, I like him, I like him a lot.

In the morning Mama's gone, and Mama's best friend Dorothy is bustling around the kitchen.

"Where's Mama?" I ask, squinting against the brightness of the morning.

"Gone," says Susan, eating Cheerios.

"Your mother is getting married," says Dorothy, picking me up and swinging me onto a chair.

"To who?"

"Mr. Smith, dummy! Who else?" says Susan.

"*I'm not dumb!*" I yell, and Susan doesn't argue back cause I am so ferocious.

Anyway Mama and Mr. Smith got married. Married in Las Vegas. Mama called us up on the phone and told us about it. Sounded all giggly and happy. Talked to us all quick cause it was long distance. Her voice familiar and different all at once. Made me feel like there was a little bit of throw-up in my throat that wouldn't come out.

When we got off the phone Susan decided she was going to make them a cake. A white wedding cake. Two layers. But it looked more yellow to me. And something went wrong with the icing recipe. It was all runny and slippery, and the top layer kept sliding off the bottom one. Susan got all mad and stomped her foot.

"It looks lovely," said Dorothy, putting her hand on Susan's shoulder.

"It looks stupid!" Susan yelled, jerking her shoulder away. *"It's a stupid stupid cake!"*

Then she stomped into our bedroom and slammed the door.

Katie and I got the top layer to stay on. We had to use a lot of raw spaghetti noodles, but it did the trick. Only lost a couple of pieces of the cake.

I went to tell Susan, thought she'd be happy, but she wasn't. Threw a pillow at me and told me, "Get out! Get out! Get out!" So I got out, and Katie and I decorated the cake. Used three bottles of little silver balls. It looked real pretty.

Mama was away for three whole days and when she came back they were married. She had a gold ring with little flowers carved around it. I wanted to hold it, but Mama said no. Said she would not take it off. Never. That it was a symbol of their love.

"Not even when you sleep?"

"Not even when I sleep."

"Or do the dishes, or shower, or houseclean?"

"No, I will wear it always," she said, looking at Mr. Smith.

So I went in my room and I made a ring for her. A ring out of my favorite doll's hair. My Raggedy Ann. And I brought it to her.

"A ring for you, Mama."

"Oh thank you, honey, it's beautiful." And she gave me a big hug and kiss, and went back to talking all excited about her wedding with Dorothy. Didn't even put my ring on. Stuck it in her pocket.

Mama and Mr. Smith held the knife together and cut the cake, cause that's what married people do. Then they fed each other. He got icing on Mama's face so he licked it off. They were laughing cause they thought it was pretty funny.

Then we got some cake. It was pretty good, but you had to be careful not to break your teeth on the spaghetti.

The one good thing about all of this is Mama doesn't have to be a schoolteacher anymore. No more baby-sitters ever again.

"A full-time mama!" she said with a smile. And us kids danced around and around and around.

New Daddy

Mr. Smith sleeps in Mama's room now. He doesn't wear any pajamas. And Mama has decided that us kids are supposed to call him Daddy.

"He's your new daddy!" she says with a big bright smile.

"But what about our old daddy? What about him?" I ask.

"Stupid," says Susan, all superior. "He doesn't care."

"Yes he does!"

"Well if he cared so much how come he's not here? How come he let Mama get married? Huh? Huh?"

I didn't have any answers, so I turned back to Mama. "It'll hurt his feelings."

"Oh boo-hoo!" said Susan. "You're just saying that cause you're his favorite."

"Girls!" Mama was holding her temples like she was getting a headache. "Please stop." She took a big breath and rubbed her hands across her face. "Can't we just all try to be happy?"

"I'll call him Dad!" Matthew said. I could tell he wanted Mr. Smith to like him. He kept racing around on his bike fast, fast, fast. Throwing his baseball as high as he could. Looking always out of the corner of his eye to see if Mr. Smith was noticing. Noticing what a nice fine boy he was. But Mr. Smith was mostly just watching Mama. That didn't stop Matthew though. He'd just run faster, dodging this way and that. Faster and faster, until his face got as red as his hair. The doctors said he was hyperactive and I guess it was probably true, cause the only time he stopped vibrating was when he was having a real bad asthma attack and even then he would twitch a little.

"I'll call him Daddy too," squeaked Katie.

"I don't care, I'll call him whatever you want me to." And Susan went back to her book.

Mama looked at me and I looked at the floor.

"Do you need to think about it for a while?"

I nodded and went into the bedroom and sat on my

bed. And I thought. I thought about the time I got Daddy the Sunday paper, reaching way up to turn the handle of the front door. It was morning and I still had my diaper on. I had to stand on tiptoe to reach. It was hard. The door finally opened. I stepped on the front step. It was that kind of bumpy blueish purple gray concrete, with lots of little rocks in it. It was cold and kind of damp under my bare feet. The lawn was wet and the sky hazy. My diaper, warm and soggy, was falling down so I had to pull it up. Then I looked down, and there was the newspaper. Wrapped in brightly colored comics, tied with coarse brown string. I bent over and picked it up. It was kind of hard to get my arms around it, cause it was so big, but I managed. It was heavy, very heavy. Made me breathe in puffs, and lean way back. I was strong. I carried it down a very long hallway to Mama and Daddy's room. But when I finally got there the door was shut. The newspaper was slipping, and I couldn't open the door, cause my arms were full. So I started to cry, and Daddy came out and he laughed. Then he picked me up and hugged and kissed me. His cheeks were scratchy. So I snuggled my face into his shoulder, soft blue striped pajamas. He carried me to his bed and I found candy under his pillow.

But then I thought about the last time we saw him. Around six months ago. And how he had a shiny new red sports car, and an apartment with a fancy swimming pool. And how Jeremy knows how to swim and was showing off about it, and so Katie decided to go for a swim and almost drowned cause she was only two and a half. She was saved by a teenager who jumped in and pulled her out by the hair. Daddy was scared when he came back downstairs with his new girlfriend and found out what had happened, so scared that he bought her a Coca-Cola and a long string of lollipops that went all the way down to the ground. And he didn't buy any for me or Susan, when we were the ones who noticed she was swimming in the first place. And Katie wouldn't share a single one with us.

"I bet she did it on purpose," Susan muttered, and I agreed.

And then I think about how Mama talks all the time, talks real angry like, her neck and ears getting all red. Talks about how he never sends us any money, even though he has a lot cause he's a TV broadcaster. Never sends us a cent, even though the judge ordered him to, because he has one kid while Mama has four. Couldn't care less if we lived or died. He only cares about my brother Jeremy, who everybody says is the spit of him. Talks about how he has a shiny new red sports car and we just have an old Volkswagen bug that keeps breaking down. And then I think about how he didn't send me a Christmas present or a birthday present, didn't even call. And I get mad and go in and tell Mama I'll call Mr. Smith Daddy. And she gives me a big hug.

New Family

We have a big family now. First it's just Mama and us four kids, and then *splam!* Can't even turn a corner without bumping into somebody new. And the strange thing is, how it happened so fast. They got married; then four days later, Dorothy comes back. Mama gives us a quick kiss and off she hops into the Volkswagen bug with the new daddy.

"Bye-bye!" she says, waving out of the window. "Bye-bye!"

"Where are you going?" asks Matthew. But it's too late cause she's already gone.

A week later Mama and the new daddy drive up. "Honk honk," goes the car. We all run outside and there getting out of the Volkswagen is Mama, the new daddy and three pale, freckle-faced strangers. Long gangly limbs connected by lumpy joints. Hair toast-colored and straggly.

Katie and I hold on to the back of Susan's shirt. She tries to get us off, but we won't let go.

"Matthew, Susan, Anna, Katie," Mama chirps brightly, "I'd like you to meet Nick, Faith and Joy, your new brother and sisters!"

"They are going to live with us now," says the new daddy.

"Where are your suitcases?" asks Matthew. "Don't you have any clothes?"

But they don't answer. The two older ones just stare

at us blank-faced. And Joy the littlest one looks like she's gonna cry.

"Give each other a hug and kiss," says the new daddy. So we do. Arms out stiffly from our sides, careful not to touch bodies.

Then we all go inside. "Would you like to see my toys?" Walking careful. Company voices. Aching tummies.

"Don't you have any toys?" says Matthew, bouncing around like he's on a pogo stick. A normal question, I think, but Faith the oldest girl, the twin, swings around on him, eyes narrow, fists clenched.

"Shut up!" she says. "Why don't you just shut up!" And Matthew's mouth drops right open, cause he was just trying to be friendly.

And from that moment on Faith had it in for him.

"Can't stand his little whiny wheezing guts!" she'd say. And I'd be glad it wasn't me she hated.

She stole Matthew's pillow and peed all over it. And Mama didn't even get mad at her or make her give it back. She just said Faith was jealous cause she didn't have a mama that loved her, and we had to give her time.

So now Faith has a pillow and Matthew doesn't. And he can't sleep without a pillow.

I offered him mine, but he said no, that she'd just steal that one and piss all over it too.

Pearl

The apartment was just too crowded, and besides Daddy likes living in the country. So we moved to a house in Klamath County. I like the country too. It's all dry and dusty, with tall tufts of parched grass. And little scatterings of crooked thirsty trees. And you can run and run and run and never bump into anyone. Not like Portland, all gray and pavement with grown-ups always squashing you in, stepping on your feet. And in the country you can get real dirty and nobody cares and you can run around without any clothes on. We make mud pies and play hide-and-seek and everything. I like it. And I even went to kindergarten for a little while.

I took the bus. A yellow school bus. It was a mini-bus cause there aren't many kids out this far.

I waited down at the bottom of the driveway with all my brothers and sisters. All of them except for Katie. Cause she's too small. And she'd cry and say, "I wanna go to school too! I wanna go to school!"

And I'd say, "No. You can't go to school, cause you're too little." And it felt good.

At school we colored and counted and played games. I loved the smell of school. The smell of chalk and paints and soap.

I planted a seed in a plastic cup with my name on it,

and it was growing. I printed my name on the cup all by myself.

There was a girl in my class named Pearl. Pearl had this special petticoat that made her dress stick straight out, and shiny black shoes you could see your face in. Toffee-colored corkscrew curls that bounced up and down when she moved, like a million tiny yo-yos.

When Pearl's daddy picked her up from school he swung her around and around, and she'd laugh and laugh. And then he pulled her in close and they hugged and kissed and rubbed noses.

Once, instead of following the line of kids to the bus, I hid behind a bush and then followed Pearl and her daddy home. I followed at a distance so they wouldn't see me.

She held his hand and skipped beside him. White tights flashing, curls bobbing.

She was talking lots, but I couldn't hear what she was saying. And every once in a while he'd smile down at her and say something. Probably how much he loved her and would never leave her and how she was the most special daughter in the whole wide world.

Their house was white. Gleaming white with green window frames and door. It was a tall house, two stories, with a real lawn, not shaggity old grass. And flowers too. All around the house and up the walkway.

Skip, skip, skip, up the walkway she went. Skip, skip, skip, up to the big green door with the shining gold knocker. Skip, skip, skip, through the door onto the plush sea-foam carpet in the hallway and then *thud!* The door swung shut and it was silent.

I stood there shifting my weight from foot to foot.

Shoes dusty and worn, knees dirty, dress hanging limply around my legs.

And then slowly I turned around and went back to school, chest hurting like it was gonna burst.

The next day I stole all my sisters' petticoats. I hid them in a big grocery bag. And when I got to school I snuck into the bathroom and put them on. They weren't sticky-out ones, but I figured with five of them, it ought to do the trick. Some were too big, so I had to roll the waistbands over a bit. Quite a bit actually. Made me look kind of fat. But I didn't care. My skirt stuck out now. Not quite like Pearl's, but almost as good.

I went to class thinking nobody would even recognize me, cause I looked so beautiful. I thought maybe they'd think I was a new girl.

But they recognized me, and bigmouth Lisa said I was trying to copy Pearl, and everyone laughed at me, even Pearl. So I left. I sat in the bathroom until school was over. Locked the door. Wouldn't come out, even when Mrs. Morgan asked me to.

So now I don't go to kindergarten anymore, cause I don't want to. And Mama and Daddy say it's okay. As a matter of fact I think Daddy's kind of proud of me dropping out in kindergarten, since he's a high school dropout himself.

Daddy's Teeth

Daddy has decided that I am the best false-teeth cleaner of the family. I feel sort of mixed about it. Since I'm the best, I'm the one who always has to clean them . . . and it kinda turns my stomach.

Around once a week he calls me. "Come here, Anna," he says. "Hold out your hands, I have a present for you." Then he spits his teeth into my hands. It's always strange to see those teeth come flying out of his mouth, strands of saliva trailing after. His face sort of caves in, and you could stick your finger right in his mouth and it wouldn't even hurt you. He also likes to grab my arm and munch on it, leaving slimy slobbery snail tracks up and down my arm. I scream cause I can't help it. He thinks I'm screaming cause I like it, but I don't.

Then I take his teeth into the bathroom to brush them. I have to walk very slowly and carefully when I have them, cause they are very, very expensive and I would be in big trouble if they broke.

His teeth are all slimy and they stink. I try to breathe real shallow and through my mouth so the smell won't get in. I use a special brush for his teeth. It is short and has very hard bristles, which is a good thing, cause his teeth are always really caked. I have to scrub and scrub to get all the yellow gunk off, and use lots and lots of soap and water. And I'm not talking about gunk just on the teeth either. Inside and out, the gums, roof, teeth ridges. Usually there's a layer of kind of goopy pasty yellowish white, and underneath is harder crusted stuff. That's the stuff that's hard to get off. My stomach really turns over when I brush his teeth, but I try to turn my stomach off and just concentrate on the job at hand.

When I'm done the teeth aren't slimy yellow or stinky anymore. They are white and pink and smooth. My stomach relaxes. I carry them back to Daddy. He puts them in his mouth and slip-slides his lips and tongue all over his teeth. "Ahhh, nice and slippery," he says, and I feel a strange sort of pride.

Faith

I was up in the attic playing with Faith.

I wasn't crazy about her choice of game. But I went along with it, cause she's not the kind of person you want to get mad at you. And on the up side, she's usually pretty fair. And after I play torture with her, she'll usually play ballet dancers with me.

This time, however, I was feeling a little uneasy. Usually she'd make me pee in a cup, eat dirt or spank me, things like that. But this time she tied my hands behind my back and then slung a rope over one of the rafters in the attic. Hung me by my neck.

I didn't die or anything, cause I gripped in my chin real tight, so the rope went around my jawline instead of my throat and I could still breathe.

She asked me if I was okay before she let go.

I couldn't talk cause then my jaw would move and the rope would choke me. So I just made a "ngh" noise in my throat and smiled.

I was a little scared, but I wasn't going to let her know it.

She let go and I swung softly back and forth, the tip of my big toe just grazing the floor.

"Are you all right?"

The rope was really digging in. But I made the noise anyway and tried to smile. Faith was really happy then. She started dancing around, her hair flapping around her face like an old hat. Faith dancing away, waving a pair of Mama's black stockings, pretending they were a whip. Whipping me with those stockings and hissing through her teeth. "You're bad, bad, bad!" Me strung up by my neck in the dirty old attic, my neck and shoulders shaking with the effort to keep the rope around my chin.

And then I heard Mama.

"Anna."

Faith froze.

"Anna!" Mama called again.

"Uhhnn," I say, wiggling.

Faith unties me and I run downstairs.

"Time for your piano lesson," says Mama. And for the first time in my life I am happy to bang away. Mama stands beside me. Her smell so familiar, a combination of milk and powder and sweat. Her hand on my shoulder, warm and loving. I start to play my scales, but then it hits me, wave after wave, and I can't go on.

"What's wrong?" asks Mama.

But I can't speak, my throat is all choked up.

Susan's Pajamas

Faith and Joy were in the doghouse.

What had happened was, Mama had found little jagged holes in Susan's pajamas. Mama said the holes were caused by someone viciously jabbing scissors into them. That the person who did this wanted to murder Susan.

It sounded pretty fascinating, but I don't know . . . It looked more like the old washing machine was eating holes in the clothes again.

Well there was a big family conference. Mama and Daddy looked into each one of our faces carefully, and held the pajamas right in front of us.

I guess Faith and Joy didn't do too well, cause now they were in the doghouse. And it couldn't be too comfortable either, cause that doghouse isn't very big.

The thing about someone being in trouble is the rest of us get to eat better.

While the bad person only gets to eat peanut butter

sandwiches, breakfast, lunch and dinner, the rest of us get treats. Like a bit of ice cream, or an eighth of a cantaloupe, or a quarter of a day-old doughnut.

Well today Mama drove into town and bought us some day-old doughnuts. And we didn't just get a quarter of a doughnut. We got a half! The catch was, Mama made us stand in front of the doghouse and eat it. It was hard to do. I don't really like doughnuts all that much.

Mama and Daddy were mad I guess, cause Joy and Faith wouldn't confess.

They kept just crying and saying, "I didn't do it. I didn't do it."

They lived in that doghouse for three weeks. We weren't allowed to say a word to them. And Daddy went down every morning and night with his belt.

Finally Faith confessed that she did it.

We had a big going-away party for her. A bonfire with hot dogs and two bags of marshmallows. And after we ate, Faith said she would give us piggyback rides.

I was first and it was fun. Faith gave good piggybacks, cause she was big and strong, and she went fast.

After I got off, Katie was acting mysterious. She said in a loud voice, "Anna, wanna marshmallow?" Now when we have a hot dog roast, we don't have to have marshmallows *offered* to us. We just take them. So I knew she meant something.

I walked over to her and we huddled by the fire.

"Faith's back," she whispered. "Faith's back is striped, striped like a zebra."

She asked me if I wanted to see. My stomach lumped over, sick but excited. I knew I shouldn't want to. But I did.

Katie and I arranged that she would get a piggyback from Faith. And when she got on her back, she would hike up Faith's shirt so I could see.

Faith said she'd be happy to give Katie a piggyback. I think it made her feel important that Katie made such a big noisy fuss about wanting one from her.

When Katie jumped on she hiked up Faith's shirt. Faith winced. I guessed it hurt to give all those piggyback rides.

She kept trying to get an arm loose and yank her shirt down. But every time she got it down, Katie would hike it up again.

All of a sudden Faith got quiet. Then she said, "That's enough piggyback rides."

She sat by the fire, real quiet like. Hunched up in a little ball. Hugging her knees and pretending to look at her feet.

She stayed like that for a long time.

The next morning she left, and I thought everything would go back to normal. "Come on, Joy, let's go play," I said, all happy and friendly. Glad we could talk again.

But she just shook her head and started to cry.

"What? What is it?"

But she just cried harder. So I put my arms around her and patted her back until she calmed down and was just hiccuping. Then all of a sudden this thought hit me: "Joy, did *you* do it?"

"No." She started crying again. "I didn't do it, but neither did Faith."

"Then why did she say she did?"

Now not only were huge wet tears streaming down her face, but snot was too. Lots of it! I'd never seen so much snot come out of one person's nose in all my life. But she didn't seem to notice, just kept on bawling. Saying it was all her fault Faith got sent away. That Faith had said she could stand the lickings but she couldn't take seeing Joy getting hit anymore. Enough was enough. She was going to put an end to all this beating.

"But it *didn't* put a end to it," wailed Joy, "cause when she said she did it, Daddy just beat her ten times as much for not confessing earlier."

I hugged Joy some more and tried not to get her snot on me. And then when she stopped crying, I went and told the others.

"Where do you think Faith went?" I asked.

"Our mom's," said Nick.

"Oh." I didn't envy Faith. I'd only met their mom once, but I didn't like her. Faith had punched me in the stomach, hard too. And I went to their mom, cause she was supposed to be watching us. I was crying and I told her what had happened and she just looked at me, as cold as cold can be, and said, "Tough titties," just like that! "Tough titties" and turned away. It made me feel uncomfortable to have a grown-up talk to me like that. Nope, I don't envy Faith going to live with her one little bit.

Pooh Pie

Daddy was off painting again. So Nick decided since he was the oldest, he was the man of the house. He started yelling at us to clean up the house, that it was a pigpen! To be quiet cause we were making too much noise! As if noise ever bothered him before! Bossing us, bossing us, bossing us. And if we didn't do as he said, he'd sock us! Well, we decided we weren't gonna take no more!

Joy, Katie and me met down by the old apple tree to carry out our plan.

Now we make mud pies. I'm not just talking about ordinary mud pies, I'm talking about beautiful mud pies, with flowers, grass, rock salt and things. Probably the world's most beautiful mud pies.

At first we thought we would make a mud pie, a beautiful mud pie, so beautiful and delicious-looking that Nick would eat it. But then we came up with an even better idea . . . *a pooh pie!* Can you imagine his face!

Now a pooh pie sounds like a good idea, but it's a lot harder than you'd imagine. The first thing is the hardest, and the most important. That part alone took most of the morning, cause as you know, it is quite difficult to just pooh on demand. I poohed, and Joy poohed, but Katie just couldn't. I was kinda mad. I don't think she tried hard enough. Anyway we couldn't wait all day, so we had to go ahead with the pooh we had. It would just be a smaller pie.

Fresh pooh steams. I didn't know that cause I'd always poohed in toilets, and I'd never seen steam coming out of a toilet. But when you pooh on a plate, it steams. It's warm too. It would be a lot more fun to make pooh pies if it wasn't for the smell.

Well we made that pooh pie and decorated it with the most beautiful flowers and leaves and rock salt. It seemed almost a shame to waste it on Nick. When it was done, we squatted around in a little circle, rocking back and forth on our heels, admiring our work. We all agreed it was the most beautiful pie that had ever been made.

We picked it up tenderly on a plate of leaves and carefully carried it to a place where Nick always liked to go and sit when he came home from school.

Then we hid in the bushes and waited.

But when Nick came home he didn't eat it. He said, "What's that stink?" And then went "Sniff . . . sniff . . ." with his nose. "Sniff, sniff . . . Sniff, sniff." And then he found it. And he went "*Aahhhyeck!* Jesus Christ!" And he kicked it with his foot. He kicked it and kicked it until it was really far away. Then he scraped his shoe in the dirt. Scraped and scraped until there was a huge cloud of dust.

It was pretty funny.

Mr. McDougle

Joy forgot to bring something for sharing, so she told her class about our pooh pie. Everybody laughed and laughed and the teacher liked the story so much she made Joy tell it to a man who came to visit the school, Mr. McDougle, so he came to see us.

Mama cleaned and cleaned. And we got dressed in good clothes.

Mr. McDougle drove an old blue car. We could see the dust cloud before we actually saw the car.

"He's coming, Mama! He's coming!" we shout and Mama's hand flies up to her hair and smoothes it. We hear the car door shut.

"Go sit on the sofa," says Mama, and we do. She moves from the window to the middle of the room.

"Knock . . . knock . . ." on the door. And us kids look at each other, cause Mama's not moving. Just standing there in the middle of the room. "Knock . . . knock . . ."

"I'm coming." She rubs her palms on her navy-blue dress with white trim, puts on her smile and walks to the door.

He is tall with rounded shoulders, brown-gray hair, beard and sandals. "Mrs. . . . Smith?" He has a nice smile. "I'm Mr. McDougle."

"Hello. Jean Smith." She shakes his hand. "Umm . . . would you like a cup of tea?"

"That would be wonderful. It's quite a drive out here." He peers past Mama at us kids on the sofa. "Hello there. Hi, Joy." A big happy smile fills Joy's face. She wiggles excitedly and waves. "I told you he was nice," she whispers to me.

And he was nice, real nice. Mama liked him too. Apparently he went to the university in the same town as Mama, so they talked a lot about Radcliffe this and Harvard that. Finally he looked at his big round watch and jumped up like he'd sat on a tack. "Ack! I'm late! Gotta be going!" He shook Mama's hand and said not to worry, no problems here, and then he left. Mama was happy.

When Daddy came home from courthouse painting in Eugene he wasn't too happy to hear about Mr. McDougle. Started yelling about the evils of schoolteachers, social workers, bureaucracy and the system and stuff. Said Mr. McDougle better not show his face around here again or else. Which is too bad, cause he seemed nice.

Moving

We've moved again. See, Mama's got a thing about social workers ever since that one in Klamath tried to get us taken away and we had to move to that big white house in Medford that we couldn't afford. And go to school every day. And smile all the time to everybody, even when our cheeks were sore. Actually, other than the smiling, I didn't mind living there. The white house was real pretty, and big too. Just like normal people, with lots of wide-open rooms. Painted pale pastel colors, with white window frames. Sunshine streaming in. And we had a veranda, and two lawns, front and back, with a fence. And there was a space in between our fence and the neighbor's fence, which was our hideout. With a board, a board that was loose on the neighbors' side. And we'd sit crouched in the overgrown grass, peering through a knothole. Tall, tough grass, coarse like a cat's tongue, and sharp too. Real sharp, it would cut you if you weren't careful or moved too fast. So we'd squat Indian style with cramps in our legs until the coast was clear. Then we'd push the board aside and sprint to the peach tree. The golden peach tree. Hearts choking us, and snatch one, two, whatever there was time for, snatch, grab and then race back. Back to the safety of our hideout. Slam the board shut. Lean against it hard just in case. Panting, pale, wide-eyed at our own badness.

Then once we were sure no one was following, we'd

divide up the small sweet peaches, covered in thick scratchy fuzz that made your mouth and throat itch. Gobble them up, faces flushed, slurping up rivulets of juice. Hot dusty days between two fences, swollen bellies full of stolen fruit.

But anyway, we left that house, cause there was a new paint contractor in town that kept underbidding Daddy, and so we just couldn't afford it. Now the house in Eagle Point was different. It was ugly but cheap, and all the neighborhood kids wore hand-me-down clothes, so you didn't feel out of place. But we had to move again, because of this social worker. And Mama was mad. Real mad. Said we'd just moved and now here we were moving again, all because of that stupid nosy woman. Mama didn't like her cause she didn't follow the rules. Normally when the social workers come, they make an appointment, you know, a certain time to come. And then we'd race around and clean the house from top to bottom, take a bath, put on school clothes, brush our hair, and if Matthew had bad asthma he'd have to go out and wait in the bushes by the creek until they left.

When the social worker left we would have a celebration, and whoever did real good got a treat, some ice cream or a piece of candy. And Mama and Daddy would talk about it and talk about it. Who did well. Said "Yes, ma'am," "No, ma'am," things like that. Who talked about how happy we were, how our Mama and Daddy loved us very much. Once I talked about how full I was from the big enormous lunch I just ate. So I got a piece of candy! A wild cherry Life Saver! But Joy got peanut butter sandwiches for dinner, cause when the social worker asked her to sit down and talk to her, Joy said she couldn't sit cause her bum was too sore, but she'd be happy to stand and talk to her instead. Joy didn't understand it, she thought she was being accommodating, but she was just being bad.

Matthew always said to me, Susan, Nick, whoever would listen, that one day he was going to come bursting out of those bushes and show them his asthma, and Mama and Daddy would get in trouble and have to give him asthma medicine, whether they believed in it or not. But he never did. He'd just stay there wheezing and gasping in the bushes until they went away.

Now that's what normally happened. But not with this social worker. She'd just pop by any old time, with her mousy hair and her big thick glasses. "Just happened to be in the area," she'd say oh so casual. "Just happened to be driving by . . ." And then she'd smile at us kids real friendly. And we'd smile back. Real big smiles and hide our dirty hands behind our backs.

It got so that Mama'd never know when she'd show up, and we were wearing school clothes every day. So finally we just upped and moved. But I don't mind. It's not like I loved that house so much, not like the white house.

Abby Road

I like this house pretty much. Mama and Daddy got the bedroom, the boys got the woodshed, and all us girls get to sleep in the attic cause it's really big. We divided it out into sections. Then we played one-potato-two-potato, and I won. So I got the window!

The house is brown. Not painted brown, it just is, cause that's the color of the wood. And it has a silver roof like a barn. And a fish pond and an old stagecoach and mistletoe trees. And Sprague River, the closest town, is around thirty miles away! So no more social workers! They wouldn't even think to drive out this far.

But the very best thing about this house, is that Daddy brought us a baby deer. He found it when he was driving home. His car hit the mama deer and killed it, and the baby deer wouldn't leave its mama. Just stayed in the middle of the road. And Daddy was scared that someone would come along and kill it, so he picked it up and brought it home.

It was a baby girl deer. Real cute. Brown with cream-colored polka dots all over her back. Big, big eyes, tiny black hooves and a wet black nose.

We named her Abby Road, and made her a home in the bathroom. She seemed to like that room the best. Maybe she liked it cause of the linoleum, cause she could slip-slide all over it like an ice skating rink. Sometimes she would wobble, slide and then lose her balance completely, and *splat!* Flat on the floor, like one of those fancy rugs you see.

There was a big white old bathtub in the bathroom. It had metal claw feet. And she liked living in the space between the bathtub and the wall. She had to squeeze a bit to get in, but once she was in, she'd stay there for hours. A curled-up shaking ball of fur. We figured she was shaking cause she was cold and missed her mama. So Katie gave Abby Road her blanket. The one she'd had since she was a baby. And we made Abby Road a little nest. And after a couple of days she stopped shaking.

At first we fed her with a baby bottle. We cut a big hole in the nipple so she could get the milk out more easily. Powdered milk, but we mixed it stronger than we made ours. Thicker, so she'd get lots of nutrients. And she liked it. She'd follow me around the kitchen while I fixed it. Skidding on her little spindly legs. Butting me with her head to make me hurry up.

When I fed her, I had to hold on to the bottle with both hands, cause she'd pull and tug on it. Sucking so vigorously that if I accidentally let go she'd probably swallow the thing whole! Slurping on the bottle, big sloppy sucks, milk escaping her greedy mouth, running in little trickles down her neck. And all the while, she'd gaze up at me with her big grateful eyes.

When she got old enough to eat grass, we started using a bowl for milk instead. Milk three times a day. And then gradually we weaned her down to one, cause milk's pretty expensive. But sometimes when Daddy wasn't looking, we'd sneak her some more.

She liked her milk, but best of all she liked Life Savers. She wasn't picky, any flavor would do, but she was especially partial to wintergreen. She would do anything for a wintergreen. Anything. Even walk on her hind legs. And if you tried to sneak one when she was anywhere near, she'd smell it on your breath and nuzzle and butt you with her head until you gave her one. And she wouldn't take no for an answer, so if you only had one, you'd have to eat it real far away and then rinse your mouth out. Either that or bite it in half and share it.

Mona and Jimmie

Daddy met a bunch of people in the park, across from one of the courthouses he was painting. Hippies. They were gathering up the autumn leaves and dancing in them. So he brought them home to show Mama. They brought wine and guitars. They stayed for around a week until we had no more food and they had no more wine and everybody was laughed out and then they left again.

All of them left but Mona. Mona and Jimmie, her little boy. Mona had long thick straight black hair with a bang cut right across her forehead. Heavy, heavy eyebrows, that never ended, one ran right into the other.

She slept with Mama and Daddy, and in the morning she would huddle up naked by the wood stove. Cold. Cold trying to get warm. Squatted down by the fire, dripping wet gray snail tracks on the floor. A large triangle of hair, curly and dark, almost black like her eyebrows. Her breasts different than Mama's. Not so used or something.

She didn't talk much. Stayed with us for about a month, and then she went. Leaving Jimmie her little boy behind.

Mama and Daddy said we had a new little brother. And that he was their little boy now, and they were his new Mama and Daddy.

But he just cried and cried and said he wanted to go with his mommy.

Katie and I were in charge of his diapers. He was almost three and he still wore diapers. Stinky diapers. Not just pee. *Pooh* too! Real stinky. And nothing we could do would make him go in the toilet. We tried everything. Asking him nicely. Asking him mean. Spanking him! Finally we got the idea of rubbing his nose in it. Just like we do with the kitties. Every time he went pooh in his diaper, we'd take it out and rub it on his nose and say, *"No, Jimmie!"* And then make him put the rest of it in the toilet. And if he took the pooh off his nose, we'd just put it back on and get him in real bad trouble.

Jimmie walked around with dried-up pooh on his nose for three days, and then finally he went in the toilet. We were real happy, and let him wash the pooh off his nose, and made him a batch of cookies. He ate them and we helped. They were good. A little salty but good.

One thing I'll say for Jimmie, is he just doesn't give up. Like the pooh for instance. Somebody put pooh on my nose, I'd get the message right quick. But no, Jimmie needs to wear it for three days! And his mama. I mean she left. She's gone. And yet every time a car drives up, he gets all excited and races to the window thinking it's her. And it isn't. Never is. But there he goes day after day tearing to the window yelling, "Mommy! Mommy!" Like this time it's really going to be her. And I wish he'd stop. I tell him, "She's gone. Your mama's gone and she's never coming back." But he just crosses his pudgy little arms across his chest and says, "Mommy loves Jimmie." And I get a knot in my stomach and it makes me feel grouchy.

Two

Vaccinations

We were all going down to the community hall to get vaccinated. You have to get vaccinated, otherwise you could catch a disease and get sick and maybe die.

I'd never been vaccinated before. None of us had.

Except Mama. She was vaccinated. And Daddy too. Although maybe not, cause he doesn't believe in doctors.

Once I cut my finger. I was slicing cheese with a big butcher knife, making a cheese sandwich, and I had to press down really hard cause the cheese was frozen to keep it fresh. And when I was pressing the knife slipped and cut my middle finger on my left hand. Right at the top. And deep too. I ran to the bathroom, blood trailing behind me, and stuck my finger under the cold-water faucet. But it wouldn't stop bleeding. It just kept bleeding and bleed-ing, splattering blood all over the white enamel tub.

When Mama came in and saw the blood she got all white and decided to take me to the doctor's.

We tiptoed out of the house with a big towel wrapped around my hand. We didn't tell anybody. Just jumped in the car and drove like lightning to the doctor's.

It was very dramatic.

The doctor's office wasn't quite as much fun. To start with, he didn't seem too alarmed by my injury. "Oh, you have a little cut," he said. "Nothing a few stitches can't take care of."

"A few *what?*"

"Stitches," he said, like he was talking about the weather. He opened up a drawer, all businesslike, and got out a needle and thread and started threading the needle. Tied a knot in it and everything. Then he grabbed my hand, clamped it down and started sewing me! Not a how do you do, or an if you please, he just sewed my finger with thick black thread.

It hurt.

And then Mama had to go away to visit Grandmother and Daddy was supposed to take me to the doctor to get my stitches out. But he wouldn't. He just tossed me a pair of tweezers and said, "Take 'em out yourself."

That's how much he doesn't believe in doctors.

He probably hadn't been vaccinated.

There was a big line of people waiting at the com-munity hall. I guess cause it was a good deal, cause these vaccinations were free. The doctor had a whole big box of them. You had to eat a sugar cube and then he would stamp you with this thing.

Nick was the first of us to go. Came back sucking on his sugar cube. Swaggering a little.

"No problem," he said. "Felt nothing. Just a little pinprick."

"Pinprick?" quavered Susan. "*A pinprick?*"

"No, more like a little tiny mosquito bite!" he said hastily. "See, nothing!" And he rolled up his sleeve to show her.

"*Blood!*" she screamed. We all crowded around, and sure enough, there glistening on his arm was a small ruby red drop of blood.

Well Susan was next in line and there was no way she was going. Mama had to drag her up, with Susan crying, "*No! No! No!*" And when he gave her the shot she started screaming, "*Ow! Ow! Ow! It hurts! It hurts!*"

It was my turn next, and she was right, it *did* hurt. It really hurt. So I cried too. The doctor was sweating all over and he shook me by my arm, my sore one, and said between clenched teeth, "Shut up, you little brat!" But that just made me cry even louder.

By the time our family left all the kids in the hall were crying and Mama's face was real red.

On the way home Mama bought Joy a soft ice cream cone, cause she was the only one who didn't embarrass the family. And Nick said, "What about me? I didn't cry!" But Mama glared at him and said the whole thing was his fault. Which I don't think was fair. I mean I don't care if I get a soft ice cream cone or not. I don't even like them. But Nick does. And Nick wasn't bad! He was brave!

Daddy's Ten-Dollar Bill

In the summer we sleep outside cause the attic's too hot. And we get to stay up late too, cause there's no school.

So we set up our sleeping bags and then we race around like crazy. Playing freeze tag, mother may I, electricity, kick the can, whatever, until it gets too dark, or we get too tired, and then we collapse into our sleeping bags, slap at mosquitoes and tell stories.

Sometimes if the mosquitoes are really bad, I try to sleep with my head under the covers. All the way under. Cause they'll bite right through your hair.

It's kind of hard to breathe under the covers. I usually don't last very long, cause I start to panic. Think I'm going to suffocate or something. Come bursting out like an underwater swimmer. Gasping for air.

I get a lot of mosquito bites.

Joy doesn't. Gets hardly any. She can sleep with her head under the covers no problem. She sleeps with her head under the covers even when there aren't any mosquitoes. How she stands it I don't know, cause she pees the bed and her blanket really stinks. She says she doesn't mind it, says she likes it! But I think it's cause she still sucks her thumb and doesn't want us to know. Just sticks her head under the covers and sneak-sucks. Thinking we won't notice. But she doesn't fool me. She says she's stopped, but her thumb still has that callus and it looks kind of wet and slobbery all the time. Sort of long and loose. But even when we're playing outside, she doesn't get that many mosquito bites, and I do. I think my blood must be sweeter or something.

Abby Road likes it when we sleep outside. She and Betsy race around and around our sleeping bags. Around and around and around. And sometimes I swear Abby Road doesn't know what she is. Sometimes she thinks she's a dog just like Betsy. Around and around she races, even tried to eat dog food once.

I don't know if she even knows what a deer is. She's always following Nick when he goes hunting. Doesn't blink an eye when he kills them. Just looks at them kind of curiously. Nick likes taking her with him. Says she's good bait!

And sometimes Abby Road thinks she's a human.

The porch is the best place to sleep. I don't know why, cause you don't get as good of a breeze there. But we all fight over it. Maybe because it's closer to Mama and Daddy, and so you feel more safe. You know, the inside lights shining through the window, listening to their voices. It's cozy.

One night when I got to sleep on the front porch, in the morning I got up to make breakfast, and when I came back to bed, who should be there, but *Abby Road!* In *my sleeping bag!* How she got in there I don't know, but there she was, front legs hanging out over the top, just like arms. Head on my pillow, eyes closed, the whole thing, just like she was human!

I said, *"Abby Road!"* Just like that, real stern. But she just rolled one eye open real lazy and looked at me as if she was saying, "Go away and let me sleep." And then she shut her eye again. I said, *"Abby Road!"* even louder, but she wouldn't get out. Finally I had to spank her bottom. And then she got out. But she was offended.

So she went and ate Daddy's ten-dollar bill. He'd left it on the table, and when he came back into the room, she was swallowing it. Well he yelled real loud and grabbed her by the neck and jammed his hand right down her throat. I thought his big old fist going down there was going to kill her. Cut off her breathing or something, but it didn't. And he pulled that ten-dollar bill right out again!

We were lucky she swallowed it whole, cause she saw Daddy coming, and knew she wasn't supposed to be eating it. So when Daddy pulled it out, it wasn't any worse for the wear. Just a little slimy and slobbery. But we just hung it on the clothing line to dry, and then Daddy spent it, and nobody ever knew.

After that Daddy would talk about how we had to get rid of Abby Road cause "her tastes are too expensive for this family." He'd say it like a joke, laugh a little, but I could tell that part of him meant it too. So I try to keep Abby Road out of his way.

Kay's

I got two dollars from Grandma Shirly and Grandpa John. They aren't my real grandparents, only my step-ones, but they always send me two dollars for my birthday and Christmas. Regular as clockwork, even though they can't really afford it. Two dollars, two smackeroos! But this year something different happened, something *special! My dad remembered my birthday!* He never remembered none of our birthdays ever! Not even Susan's, and her birthday's on Valentine's Day, which is pretty hard to forget. Birthdays, Christmases, nothing. But all of a sudden, out of the blue, he remembered my birthday! Mine! I guess he remembered it cause he loved me. Mama always said of all the girls I was his favorite.

Everyone looked at me envious like. Not so much for the five-dollar bill, which was more money than any of us had ever had, but because all of a sudden I had a father, a real one, a blood one who loved me and remembered my birthday and sent me a brand-new crisp five-dollar bill, and a card. A card with a heart on it that said "To my birthday girl. Love, Dad." I was remembered. I was loved! I was bursting!

I danced, danced around the living room. Waving my five-dollar bill and card like banners. Banners of bravery won in the war. I knew it was selfish. Selfish to dance with my brothers and sisters watching me with hungry pinched eyes.

But I couldn't help it. I danced and danced until my feet were sore and my breath was gone. Then I staggered into Mama's bedroom. Mama was lying facedown on her bed. Lying kinda like a rag doll flung down on the bed. Crumpled, twisted, still . . .

"Mama," I said. She didn't answer.

"Mama!" Proud, determined. "I'm not going to put it in the bank!" I waited but she didn't answer . . . didn't move.

"Mama," I said louder, "I'm not going to put it in the bank." I paused, she still didn't answer, so I carried on. Louder. "I'm going to buy something. Something special!"

She still didn't speak, didn't speak or move. I knew she was mad. Mad that he wrote to me. Mad that I made such a big deal. Mad that I cared, so I left.

I wrapped my money in my fancy lady scarf and thumbtacked it to the ceiling above my bed. I lay on my bed for hours and gazed up at my money, my special money, and dreamt about what I would buy.

Then one night it hit me. It hit me like a bolt of lightning. A dress! A new dress, a brand-new dress! Not a hand-me-down old secondhand Sallyanne special! No sir! A *new* dress! A brand-new dress! *A real one!*

The very next day I washed my face and hands, even under my fingernails, brushed my hair, put on some perfume, and went down to Kay's. Kay's Fine Clothing Apparel. It was a little shop on the second floor of someone's house. I walked up the wood stairs, footsteps loud. I stood at the top of the stairs by the doorway and breathed.

Scared. Scared to go in, scared not to. Scared they would know that my clothes were secondhand, that they'd laugh at me, throw me out . . . .

Then the door opened. A lady was going out. A fancy lady, curlers and everything. She was talking to Kay over her shoulder, laughing. Holding the door open and talking about some fancy party. Then she glanced down and smiled at me and waved me inside. Kept talking to Kay, didn't say nothing about my secondhand clothes, nothing, didn't even seem to notice. Just smiled and waved me in, easy as pie. I walked in on the soft red carpet, excited, careful. Hands behind my back so they'd know I wasn't going to touch anything.

I found a section that looked like kids' dresses. But I didn't quite know how to tell if they fit or not, cause they were all jammed together on the rack. So I stood there looking at the rack of clothes, new clothes, hands behind my back. I stood there for a long time. Walking around and around the rack, sweating, trying to figure out what to do next.

"Do you need some help?" I jumped. There was Kay. I knew she was Kay cause that's what the lady called her. And I think she was the owner cause the store was called Kay's Fine Clothing Apparel. And her name was Kay and she was in the shop asking me if I needed some help. I cleared my throat. "I want to buy a dress," I said, looking at my hand-me-down shoes.

"A dress," she said. "Hmmm . . . what kind of dress?"

"A new dress," I said, "a brand-new dress."

"A brand-new dress," she said. "That's all we have here." She paused for a second and looked at me hard like she was seeing straight through all my secondhand clothes, deep inside me to my gut. Then, "How much do you have to spend?"

"Seven dollars," I said. I took my fine lady scarf out of my sister's purse that I had borrowed and opened it up and showed it to her, so she'd know I wasn't wasting her time.

She looked at it. "Seven dollars," she said. "Hmmmm . . . What size are you?"

"I don't know."

"How old are you?"

"Seven, I just turned seven."

"Seven," she said. "Hmmm . . ." She flipped through the clothing rack, the metal hangers making a clicking "eerrch" sound, flip, flip, flip. Then, "Ahhh . . . here's something, normally fifteen dollars but I was just going to put it on sale today. It's just your size and on sale for seven dollars." She held it up. It was a light blue vinyl dress with a peace sign zipper up the front. It wasn't quite what I had in mind. I had pictured a beautiful frothy dress with lace and ribbons and lots of petticoats that made the skirt stick right out. But she was standing there smiling at me, holding it in front of her, so I took it and smiled back. She took me to the dressing room and I tried it on. When I showed it to her, she seemed really excited. Said how it fit me perfect. Just perfect, like a glove, made my eyes glow. I had to admit, it did look pretty, real pretty actually. Not what I imagined, but it was pretty. And new. Brand-new, so I bought it.

I wore that dress for a long long time. It got shorter and shorter until finally it was a vest and the vinyl had brown splits and cracks running up and down it. Everybody tried to get me to throw it away. But I wouldn't. I wore it and wore it until it started leaving big red marks in my underarms.

Woodshed

When I was cooking breakfast some grease jumped out of the frying pan and into my eye. It really hurt, but the worst part was, all that grease floating around made my vision blurry, and I thought maybe I was going blind, and that's what really made me cry.

Daddy came roaring out of the bedroom, pulled down my pants and *spank, spank, spank* on my bare bottom. How did I know it was him, you might ask yourself, since I thought I was going blind. Well, I might have thought I was going blind, but I sure as heck wasn't going deaf! And even if I was going deaf, I still would have heard him cause he was yelling to beat the band!

Anyway, it *was* him, and I lost house privileges for a week for making too much noise. Which is kinda weird, cause he made more noise than me, and if he wanted me to be quieter, spanking me wasn't the way to go about it. Cause I just went out to the woodshed and yelled even louder, kicked things too, and I hope I gave him a headache!

So anyway, I didn't go blind, and had to live in the woodshed for a week. Nick and Matthew lived there all the time, cause there wasn't enough room in the house. They hated it, especially in the winter, cause there wasn't any heat. But it wasn't winter now, and I didn't mind it. Actually, it was kind of peaceful. The boys were always out and about, and only came in at night to sleep. So except for the cats and dogs, I basically had the run of the place. And a sturdy little place it was too. I mean it was old, real old, you could tell by the wood. And yet, most of the walls were up, only a few boards fallen away here and there. It was a sweet little place, with a short squat doorway and a crooked old door with a rusty hinge half falling out of the rotting wood so you had to lift up the whole door to open or shut it. And there was this little tiny window in the very top of the back wall. A little tiny cracked window, coated with cobwebs and years and years of dust. And around midafternoon, the sun would always manage somehow to peel away the grime, force its way through, and envelop the inside in warm amber light. You'd have to be there at the right moment or you'd miss it, cause it would only last around forty-five minutes tops, and then it would be over.

Another thing I discovered was dog food tastes *good!* It really does! You know how I found this out? Well you know how I burnt my eye cooking breakfast, and Daddy spanked me and sent me to the woodshed? Well I was *cooking* breakfast, not *eating* it. So I was hungry! Real hungry! But I wasn't allowed inside, and everybody inside just forgot about me, and I got hungrier and hungrier. And then all of a sudden I noticed the dog crunch-crunching on dog food, and she seemed to be enjoying it, and I was really

really hungry, so I got a piece of dog food, not from the bowl where Betsy had been slobbering dog slobber of course, I got a fresh piece from the middle of the bag, and . . . I . . . *popped it in my mouth and ate it!* And it was *good!* It had a slight salt coating on the outside and it was crunchy and tasted delicious. So I ate some more. It's a good kind of snack actually. Fills you up, keeps your teeth sharp and clean, and is good for you.

So I really liked living in the woodshed. I swept it out and made it nice and cozy. I'd probably be living there still except on the last night I woke up and Nick had crawled into my blanket. I guess maybe he was missing Faith because they were always together. Anyway he crawled into my blanket and was poking his penis into my bellybutton. And when I asked him what he was doing, he said in a very strange voice, "Look at the stars, Anna . . . What a beautiful night." Now what that has to do with him poking his penis in my bellybutton I'll never know, but anyway it made me feel funny, so I was glad my week was over, and I got to go back inside and sleep with my sisters again.

Grown-ups

Susan got to be a grown-up.

Mama and Daddy had lots of friends over. Lots of them. Mostly strangers though. Except Mark and Sasha, and Barry and Molly. I like Mark and Sasha, they're real nice. I always try to behave real well around them and be helpful so they'll get the idea to adopt me and I could be their daughter and help them when they have a baby, cause I know all about babies. You know, feeding, diapers, burping and things. So I tell them how good I am with babies, and ask them when they're gonna get married and have a baby and stuff, and they laugh and hold hands and Sasha gets all shy and red in the face, so from the looks of it, maybe soon.

Anyway, I like them, but I'm not crazy about Barry and Molly. They aren't bad really, ignore us kids for the most part. It's just at nighttime when I have to kiss the grown-ups good night, Barry always grabs a hold of me and kisses me right on the mouth. Which wouldn't be so bad if he kept his mouth shut. But he doesn't, he always opens it up and gives a long, and I mean *long* wet slobbery kiss. It's really disgusting. And I have to wipe off my mouth and face after I kiss him, even my tongue. I use the sleeve of my nightgown, but I wait until I leave the living room so I won't hurt his feelings.

Anyway we had kissed everybody good night and

were upstairs in bed. Well Susan was in bed, and the rest of us were on the floor. Actually, she was on four of them. Mattresses. We'd piled the mattresses up and put a pea under them so we could find out which one of us had royal blood in our veins. Tonight was Susan's turn, cause it was her idea, and with any luck she would be black and blue by morning. "Can you feel it?" we asked. "Can you feel it?" "Yes, yes, I believe I can," she replied. Us upstairs, giggling and whispering. The grown-ups downstairs, loud, raucous.

Then Mama came up, stood at the top of the stairs, swaying slightly, her hair down, wavy almost to her waist. Couldn't see her face though, just a silhouette, a tall silhouette against the light bulb.

"Susan," she called, tilting her head back, slightly to one side.

"Susan, how would you like to come downstairs for a while and be a grown-up?" "What, Mama?" said Susan, sitting up. "How would you like to come downstairs and be a grown-up?" Susan scrambled to her feet, giving a little jubilant hop. "Yes, Mama," she said, sliding off the bed and smoothing down her faded flannel nightgown. "Yes, Mama, I would!" "Well come on then." Mama held out her arm and Susan nestled inside it and they went downstairs together.

Susan was gone downstairs for a long, long time. I tried to stay up, but I must have fallen asleep, cause the next thing I remember, I was awake. You know that sudden awake where your eyes just pop open, and your heart's beating fast for no reason. That was how I woke up. The house was quiet. The moon coating everything with silvery blue stillness. Everything quiet, so quiet. And then I heard a noise, a muffled sobbing noise escaping from the top of the beds. "Susan," I whispered. She didn't answer so I tiptoed over to the bed. She was on her side curled up into a little shaking ball. "Susan," I whispered. "Are you okay?" She still didn't say anything, so I tried again. "Susan?"

Then all of a sudden she sat up, her dark hair whipping around her. She sat up and glared at me. "What . . . do . . . you . . . want!" She demanded ferociously. "What!" Her wet face pale, dark red lipstick smeared around her mouth, eyebrows painted in, two black slashes across her forehead, mascara running rivulets down her cheeks. "What!" She smelled of perfume and cigarettes. Her skinny body wrapped in Mama's see-through maroon negligee, a large black bra hanging loosely from her shoulders empty.

"What happened to your hair?" I said finally, cause even in the moonlight I could see that part of it had been cut and was hanging all jaggity around one side of her face. Her eyes filled up and overflowed. I started to reach out and pat her on the shoulder but I didn't, cause I was scared she'd break. So I just stood there for a while shifting from foot to foot and then I went back to bed.

In the morning, I figured out what happened to her hair. It was stuck under her arms and on her down there. The only reason I know this was cause I caught her in the bathroom trying to get it off. But it wouldn't come off, and I saw it. I tried to help her, but it was stuck there good. They must have used some awful strong glue.

Dippity-Do

We were driving over to see Jack. Jack was my stepbrother. He was grown up, and he'd just gotten married. He was nineteen years old, but he wasn't in the war. He had a bum knee. Funny you hear about people all the time trying to get out of the war. But not Jack, he really wanted to go. So we weren't supposed to mention it.

See, it was summer and we had been traveling all over the country painting highway patrol offices, and we were pretty close to where Jack lived. So, Daddy decided we should take a day off and go visit him.

I was kind of glad, cause painting highway patrol offices is hard work. I was in charge of all the radiators. See, the paintbrushes couldn't fit between the metal gaps. No one could figure out what to do . . . but me! I devised a way of painting them *with my hands!* I'd just slip my hands in the paint bucket, get them all full of gooey paint, and then slide them up and down the metal pieces! Everybody was real impressed. Even the grown-ups! So anyway, now I was in charge of all the radiators. While the other kids had to stay home at camp, I went to work with the grown-ups every day. I got to have baloney sandwiches, Tang and a cookie at lunch. Which was pretty good eating.

I was lucky. But painting all those radiators was hard. Cause as you know there are a lot of radiators in highway patrol offices. A lot.

So I was glad we were going to see my stepbrother Jack. Besides, I'd never met him before.

We bounced along in the van. Katie and Joy were squabbling behind me. It sounded like fun, but I had better things to do. I was trying to think up a profound poem. Susan just had a poem published in *Barricades* magazine. A poem about pigeons and doves, cooing and love and war and things. Mama and Daddy had sent copies to everyone they knew, and had lots of copies on hand.

Susan was famous.

Well she was only eight and a half. One and a half years older than me. And if she could do it, so could I.

I lay on the back seat of the Volkswagen van. With my shoes off and my feet pressed against the window. That way we'd look like one of those rich people's cars with decals on the windows. Feet decals! And every once in a while if I noticed somebody looking at my feet, I'd wiggle my toes a bit. Pretty funny huh? I bet they got a shock. It was lucky I guess that no one crashed.

Feet on the window, toes wiggling, I tried and tried to think of a poem . . . And finally inspiration struck!

"Mama! I thought of a *poem!*"

"Oh, good, dear . . ." she said absentmindedly. I guess she didn't realize I thought of a good one. A real good one. A profound one!

"Listen, Mama, listen . . . Children's voices singing: Vietnam, Vietnam, Vietnam is very calm . . . Man's voice: The man who killed them all is thrilled in Vietnam. Children singing: Vietnam, Vietnam, Vietnam *is* very calm *is* Vietnam!" I paused dramatically.

"Oh . . . hummm," said Mama, and went back to her book.

"Mama, Mama, aren't you going to write it down?" I looked at her expectantly. She didn't say anything. My voice started to get higher. "Aren't you going to write it down? Mama, aren't you? You always write Susan's down, Mama."

Mama sighed. "Okay . . . Get me some paper." She looked kind of tired. I guess she didn't sleep good the night before. Oh well. She wrote it down.

Jack and his wife live in a trailer park. I'd never been in a trailer park before.

It was like a little neighborhood of trailers. All kinds of trailers, all kinds of sizes. There were ones with little gardens, flowers and things. One even had a little white picket fence. I decided then and there that I was going to live in a trailer park when I grew up!

Jack wasn't there. I guess he was at work. But his wife was home. Her name was Lana. She was real pretty, curly hair and makeup.

They weren't expecting us. It was supposed to be a surprise visit. Well, she sure was surprised. I don't think she knew whether or not to let us in. There were nine of us, and her trailer was not one of the bigger ones.

I guess she finally believed Daddy about us all being related to Jack, cause she let us in.

She kept apologizing for the state of the place, but as far as I could see, it was as neat as a pin. She should get a look at our place sometime.

We all sat around on the living room floor and looked at each other, all of us that is except for Jimmie. He was charging around on his little legs pretending to be a bicycle and he kept banging into people cause it was kind of squishy. Lana talked a little about this, and a little about that. Lipsticked lips moving. Hand caressing curls. I just sat there. Inhaling her.

Mama showed her Susan's poem in *Barricades* magazine. Finally Nick piped up. "Can we go outside?" Mama looked at Lana. "Would it be all right?" Mama was putting on her civilized cultured voice, the one she uses for company. Lana said, "Sure, yeah, go ahead." She said it real quick like the words wanted to come out faster than she could form them.

Everybody left with a big ruckus and hooha. Everybody that is but me. I had decided that if I was going to look like Lana, and live like Lana, I would have to watch her for a while to learn what to do when the time came.

I said I had a headache. Mama looked tired, but I timed it well. See, Mama was being cultured and refined. Now I could tell she didn't quite believe me, but cultured and refined people don't call other people fakes or liars. So she had to pretend to believe me. And be concerned like a normal mother. She asked Lana if I could stay because I had a headache. Lana looked down at me and said, "Oh the poor little thing. Of course she can stay."

I was in heaven. Everyone else left. And I had Lana all to myself.

"I have to curl my hair before Jack gets home," she said. "But if you like you can lie on my bed and rest."

I lay on her beautiful bed. It had a pale green bedspread, with little decorated pillows.

The afternoon sun, a kind of dusky rose light, came in through the window, casting long warm beams across the room.

She sat down at a white vanity. Her back to me. I could see her reflection in the mirror. The sunlight, the clean bedspread, the smell of cosmetics, powder and perfume. And mostly Lana. Lana with the curly hair.

She unscrewed a jar of blue stuff. It was a clear blue, kind of the color of a blue cleary marble. It was goopy. She brushed out a bit of hair, dipped her fingers in the jar, then brought her fingers out all blue and goopy, rubbed it in her hair and rolled it up in a curler. I could smell it from the bed. I was so excited. I wanted to say something. But I didn't, cause I knew if I was talkative she might figure out that I was faking and I would have to go walk with the others. So I just lay there. And watched her, with half-shut eyes, through the mirror. Strand after strand of hair. Brush, goop, roll. Brush, goop, roll.

Finally she was done. In the distance I could hear the faint sounds of the family coming back. She got up quietly and started to leave the room. Quickly, before the magic was over, I asked, "What is that blue stuff you put in your hair?" She looked surprised. I guess she thought I was asleep.

"Oh . . ." She looked confused. "This stuff?" she asked, pointing at the jar. I nodded. She laughed softly. She looked so pretty when she laughed. "It's Dippity-Do." Then, still smiling, she left.

I lay there forming the words over and over again, like some sort of chant, some sort of spell that would propel me into a life like hers. Dippity-Do . . . Dippity-Do . . . Dippity-Do.

Jack

All Jack did was complain. Complain about the food, complain about us kids, complain about the work. I could have told him back at the trailer he wouldn't like it. Why would he want to leave Lana and his beautiful trailer to come with us? Painting was hard work.

We slept on the ground. At least he had a nice warm sleeping bag. Us kids just had a blanket. When it rained, there would be a scramble to sleep under the van. Usually the bigger kids won. And Katie, Joy and I would just wrap our wet blanket around us tightly and dream about the time when we would be grown-ups and get to sleep in the van when it rained, with nice warm sleeping bags.

The grown-ups ate much better than we did too. They got first dibs on everything and we got what was left over.

But anyway, with all these advantages, all he did was snort, "Some vacation . . ." Finally he stopped getting up early and going into the highway patrol to work. He just stayed at camp with the kids. And Katie told me that he'd usually stay in his sleeping bag till noon, and yell all the time, "Shut the fuck up, you little brats!" I was glad I was working. It didn't sound like much fun at camp.

Jack. I didn't like him very much. But the night he asked me if I wanted to sleep in his sleeping bag, I was excited. It was an honor to sleep in a grown-up's sleeping bag. A rare privilege! It meant you were special! Not only that, it was cozy, and a heck of a lot warmer than my holey blanket.

He unzipped part of his sleeping bag and pulled the flap back. I threw my old blanket on Katie. Scampered over and scrambled in. Ah, nice and cozy, toasty warm.

"Scoot down," said Jack in a soft gruff voice. I scooted. "More," he said. I hesitated a minute. I like to sleep with my head out in the air. Otherwise I feel suffocated. "Scoot down more or get out," he said. I scooted down. To get kicked out of a grown-up's sleeping bag would be humiliating.

It was dark down in his sleeping bag. I couldn't breathe good. It was sweaty, and with Jack so grouchy I started to wonder if it was really worth it. All this just so I could sleep with a grown-up. I longed for my old blanket, my sisters, my head sticking out. Besides I felt funny in my tummy . . . I started to cry, quietly so he wouldn't know. I guess he knew though, cause he patted my head kind of awkwardly, and said, "Don't cry, kid." I cried even harder. "Listen . . . shhh . . . listen, kid . . . Do you believe in magic?"

That stopped me in my tracks. Magic! Of course I believed in magic. I was more certain of it than I was of anything. The moon, the stars, my hand in front of my face.

And I knew, without a doubt, that it was only a matter of time before it happened to me.

"Yes," I whispered, trembling with excitement. All sadness, longing, claustrophobia gone.

"Yes, I believe in magic!"

"Shall I show you something magic? Some magic you can make happen?"

"Yes . . . yes please!" It was happening just like in the books! I was going to be given magic powers!

"Well," Jack said, "what you have to do is lick this . . . and it will grow big. And after it gets big it will turn into a lollipop!"

"Lick what? Lick what?" I asked.

"Lick . . . this."

"Lick what?" I couldn't see a thing.

"Here, let me help you." He took the back of my head and pushed it down. It sure was squashed at the bottom of that sleeping bag. But I didn't complain. I'd read books. I knew you had to have hardships before you became magic.

Then with his other hand he put something against my mouth . . . It was his *penis!* No way was I going to lick that!

But just in the nick of time I remembered that, with magic, things aren't what they seem. An ugly frog might actually be a handsome prince in disguise. And with magic, you are always being tested to see if you have the faith. Well I had the faith. So I let him put it in my mouth.

"Lick it," he whispered. So I did. And sure enough, it started to grow. I was excited and pleased. Only a little longer and I would be magic!

"Lick it faster." He sounded like he had something caught in his throat, cause his voice came out all raggity like. I stopped to tell him I was licking as fast as I could. But I didn't get it out, cause he whacked me on the back of my head and said, "Don't stop!" Then, "Shit, you aren't doing it right."

My heart sank. I was doing the best I could. Did this mean I wasn't going to get my magic?

"Here, suck it instead," he said impatiently, pushing the thing right into my mouth.

I almost choked, cause it went right down my throat. But I didn't complain. I had another chance to be magic. And knowing Jack, it was probably my last. I sucked it.

"Ummm . . . that's better . . . that's real good," he said.

I sucked and I sucked. My throat was sore, my mouth was tired. And my hair hurt where he had grabbed it and was forcing my head back and forth. Back and forth.

He must have forgot I was only seven, and my mouth wasn't that big, cause he kept jamming it real hard into my throat, almost making me throw up. I didn't know if I wanted magic this much.

All of a sudden he groaned and peed in my mouth! Enough was enough. All that other stuff I could take to get magic. *But peeing in my mouth! No way!* I spit it out and started kicking and scratching and biting and yelling. My rage building with every kick, every hit, every word. *"You peed in my mouth! You peed in my mouth! You said I was going to have magic! But I didn't! You just peed in my mouth!"*

He got real mad. He jumped out of his sleeping bag, dragged me out, and started hitting me and hitting me, saying, "Shut up, you little brat! Shut up!"

Well I didn't. I just kept hitting him back and yelling. *"I hate you! I hate you! You promised me magic and you just peed in my mouth!"*

67

He hit me and hit me and hit me until I was just lying curled up on the ground crying, "You peed in my mouth . . . you peed in my mouth."

Then he grabbed his sleeping bag. Kicked me one more time, hissed through his teeth, "Stupid fucking bitch!" and left. I lay there, hurting all over. Mad. So mad I could taste it.

. . . Well, the very next day I got my revenge . . . and boy was it sweet! I sang "The bear went over the mountain" right at him. Right to his face, and *loud!* He knew what I was talking about! Yes he did. And there was nothing he could do about it! Nothing!

Fourth of July

We drove and drove and couldn't find a good campsite. It was getting dark so . . . Mama and Daddy splurged and we stayed in a campground! Three bucks a night!

It was pretty exciting. There were numbered sections of ground where you could stay, and a cement stove to build your fire in, and a water faucet at the end of each road. There even was a *shower* with hot and cold water!

After dinner I walked down to the shower with my sisters and took a long shower, good and hot. Washed my hair and everything.

It was real cold when we got out, and we wanted to run back to camp, but we couldn't cause the road was real rough gravel, and it hurt our feet. And we couldn't see where we were going cause it was dark, so we just kind of hobble-hopped. In the beginning it was frustrating that we couldn't go fast, but then all of a sudden it was funny, cause all you could hear was "Cold . . . cold . . ." "Ouch!" "Ooph!" "Cold . . ." We laughed and laughed until our bellies were sore.

When we got back to camp we rolled up in our blankets and Susan told a story. Which was lucky, cause she told the best. Exciting adventure stories with magic in them. She made them up right out of her head, so real you could taste them. We lay on the lumpy ground, wrapped warm in our blankets, stared up at the black starry sky and listened. Somebody had a transistor radio playing softly. I could hear the rise and fall of the grown-ups' conversation. The fire crackling. Farther off, a baby crying. An owl, crickets, frogs. It was comforting, people all around, life going on, Susan telling a story . . .

The next morning it was the Fourth of July. We got up real early and dressed all in red, white and blue. Then we got our musical instruments. Lids off pans, a spoon on a can of beans, whistles. I got the big pot for a drum. The campground sure was going to be excited to have live entertainment.

We started the parade at our campsite, and then marched up and down the sections, weaving in and out of trailers and tents, banging on our instruments and singing patriotic songs.

Nick thought we were crazy. He staggered around us laughing and making kookoo faces and gagging noises. But we just ignored him and marched on singing at the top of our lungs. We sounded quite professional. Some people smiled, some people laughed and pointed, dogs followed us barking. It was quite a parade. We were the center of attention at that campsite.

Then all of a sudden a tent flap flew open and a guy stuck his head out. His hair was standing up funny like a chicken had been scratching on it. And his face was kind of smooshed on one side and he was real grouchy. "Shut up!" he yelled. What should we do? Stop because of one grouch who doesn't like parades? No! We started up louder than ever. He scrambled out of his tent and stood right in front of our parade. He was very tall and old too, maybe seventeen. "I said *shut up! Stop that racket! People* are trying to *sleep!*" Katie started to cry. "It's not a racket," Susan explained disdainfully in her fine lady voice. "It's a Fourth of July parade." "Yeeaaaaah . . ." wailed Katie. "It's a Fourth of July paraaaaaade!" "I don't care what the *fuck you call it!*" By this time Katie was howling full throttle. "It's a racket and I'm telling you to *shut the fuck up!*"

Then suddenly from behind us, there was a small defiant voice. "They don't have to if they don't want to." We all turned around, and to our amazement, there was Nick! We'd thought he'd left a long time ago. "Oh yeah?" said the bad guy. Eyes narrowing, mouth smiling. "Says who?" "Says me," said Nick in a voice quite a bit higher than his normal one. His face had gone pale, so his freckles really stood out. "Okay," said the guy. "Put up your dukes." I wasn't sure what dukes were, but I guessed it must mean fists, cause they both put up their fists and started circling around.

Nick yelled over his shoulder, "Run . . . go on! Get back to camp!"

We ran. We ran fast, stumbling over rocks we couldn't see cause we were crying.

It was a long time before Nick came back to camp. He had a black eye and a swollen lip. He was dusty all over and looked like he had been crying.

None of us talked much.

When we left, the campkeeper's daughter swung the gate open and waved and smiled. She had long blond hair down to her waist. Daddy said, "What a beautiful smile that girl has." He'd never told me I had a beautiful smile. So what made hers beautiful and mine not? I thought about her smile for a long time. Finally I realized what the difference was. She showed all of her teeth when she smiled. I practiced and I practiced. But whenever Mama saw it she'd say, "Anna, get that ridiculous grimace off your face!" real irritably. I guess she didn't want me to be beautiful.

Grandma Shirly and Grandpa John

We were visiting Grandma Shirly and Grandpa John! I love Grandma Shirly. I wish she was my real grandmother. But she's not. She's really only Nick, Faith, and Joy's, cause she's the mama of their mama.

I was a little worried before we arrived that she'd have decided she didn't love me anymore, cause I'm not her blood. But she still loved me! Hugged me and kissed me just as hard as she did Nick and Joy. I like visiting them. They're my favorite grandparents! Actually they're everybody's! They are real nice. And they have a fridge on the back porch and it's always plumb full of Cragmount soda pop! Cans and cans of it. All piled up. Every flavor under the sun! Root beer, cream soda, lemon-lime, raspberry, grape, Coca-Cola! Lots and lots! And Grandma Shirly lets us drink it! As much as we want!

"That's what it's there for," she says.

And they have a candy jar. A crystal candy jar with a lid. It's right by Grandpa John's chair that he sits in. He likes to watch TV and smoke. Watches TV all day long. All day long in his fancy chair that makes his feet go up.

We aren't allowed to sit in it cause it's just for him. It's his chair, cause he has a bad back.

It's his candy jar too. But we are allowed to have one piece when we come in to kiss him good night.

Grandma Shirly crocheted a blanket to cover his chair

and make it comfortable. She crocheted it with multicolored yarn, so it looks like autumn leaves all jumbled up.

And she cooks too! Cooks real good. Not just one thing either. Full meals, just like in the books. Last night for instance, we had fried chicken, mashed potatoes, gravy, green peas, homemade biscuits, and strawberry shortcake for dessert. With real whipped cream! She makes the best food I ever tasted. And when I tell her, she smiles and says it's all the love she cooks it with that makes it taste so good.

We get to eat as much as we want. She doesn't mind, Grandma Shirly *likes it* when we eat a lot!

She's soft and quiet. Wavy brown and gray hair, parted on the side, just brushing the bottom of her ears. Lots of lines on her forehead, and around her eyes. A kind of sadness, I don't know why.

Grandma and Grandpa have a color TV. And we're allowed to watch it. Which is what I was doing. Lying on the floor, pink cream soda in my tummy, watching TV. *Bewitched*. It's a real good show about this blond lady who's a witch. A nice one. And she's married to this skinny man with dark greasy hair, and he doesn't like it when she uses witchcraft. I don't know why, cause if I was him, I'd want her to use it all the time. Anyway, it's a real funny show. I was laughing my guts out when Grandpa John came in.

He switched the channel to boxing and then stepped over me and sat in his chair and lit up a cigarette. He didn't smoke Salem menthols like Daddy. Said menthols were for sissies. Smoked plain old Camels. Unfiltered.

He smoked a lot. Didn't take long for him to fill up a room with his smoke. Big ol' clouds of it.

I didn't leave when he switched the channel. Even though I don't like boxing, cause it wouldn't be polite.

I could see him out of the corner of my eye, kind of looking at me funny. I figured it must have been cause I was too close to his chair, so I scooted farther away.

"Whatcha doing?" he asked, still looking at me.

"Giving you a better view."

"My view's fine. Come here, come on . . . Bring that stool and sit by me."

So I got Grandma's footstool and sat by him. I felt pretty special sitting on Grandma's footstool. She'd made the cushion by herself. Needlepoint.

He brought his big old hand up and patted me on the head.

"Pretty hair," he said.

"Thank you." I was glad I'd remembered to brush it that morning.

"You like boxing?"

"Yes," I said.

"Me too."

We sat there for a while in silence. "Thunk . . . thunk . . . thunk . . ." One guy was really hitting the other guy. Once or twice in the stomach, but mostly in the face. "Thunk . . . thunk . . . thunk . . ."

Grandpa John smoking.

He reached over and took a sweet out of the jar and gave it to me. A rum and butter.

"You're a good girl," he said, patting me on the head. "I betcha know how to keep a secret, don't cha?"

I nodded cause my mouth was full of toffee.

"You want me to show you something? A secret just between you and me?"

I nodded.

"Well come on then." He put out his cigarette and got up. He had to push with both of his hands on the armrests.

"Turn off the TV, will you?"

I ran over and turned it off.

"There's a good girl. Okay, come on."

"Where are we going, Grandpa?" I asked.

"Shhh . . . quiet," he whispered, putting a finger to his mouth. "We don't want your grandma to know." He winked at me and we both tiptoed out of the house. Snuck out the back door, held the screen door so it wouldn't slam shut.

Once we got out of the house he looked all around and then walked real fast across the lawn. Faster than I'd ever seen Grandpa John walk before. I had to run to keep up.

When we got far enough away from the house he slowed down. He wasn't looking at me though.

"Where are we going, Grandpa?" I asked. He didn't answer, so I asked him again. "Where are we going, Grandpa?"

"To see the skunk cabbage," he said, still not looking at me.

"What's skunk cabbage, Grandpa?"

Now he stopped. Looked at me.

"Don't cha know what skunk cabbage is?"

"No." I shook my head. "I've never seen it before."

"I bet you have . . . I bet you've seen lots of it . . . seen it all your life. Just didn't know that's what it was."

"What's it look like, Grandpa?"

He laughed. I wasn't sure what I'd said that was so

funny, but he laughed so hard that his eyes got wet and made him cough. He coughed a deep raggity cough, all choked up with spit. Doubling up his long angular body.

When he finished he wiped his eyes and took me by the shoulders and looked right into my eyes.

"Well little girl," he drawled. "Skunk cabbage looks like a flower . . . a beautiful flower. And that's what you'd think it was just looking at it. A flower. But," he said slowly, rolling the words off like he was tasting them. Bringing his face closer and closer. "But . . . when you get close . . . when you get close to them, these skunk cabbages . . . you find out that . . . they stink. They stink real bad . . . just like people."

Then he let go of me and started walking again. Didn't look back. I was kinda scared. Didn't know what to do, so I followed him.

He didn't talk to me again. It was like he was mad or something.

We got to the skunk cabbages and he stopped. I could tell they were the skunk cabbages cause they stank. Smelled kind of like a skunk. I guess that's why they're called that.

"Sit down," he said.

So I sat down. The ground was moist. I could feel it soaking through the seat of my pants.

Then Grandpa unzipped his pants, took out his penis and started shaking it. At first he was looking right at me, then he forgot about me and rolled his eyes up, like he was trying to see what the inside of his eyelids looked like. Shaking his penis, shaking and pulling on it. Then he peed. Put his penis back in his old blue jeans and turned around and started walking home.

Walked fast.

I had to run so I wouldn't get lost.

He didn't talk to me.

When we got back home he went straight to the TV. Turned it on. More boxing. Boxing, TV and his cigarettes. Smoking his cigarettes, sitting in his chair.

I went to the back porch to get a soda. Maybe grape. But when I passed the kitchen someone grabbed my arm and pulled me into the pantry.

When my eyes adjusted to the dark, I could see that it was Grandma Shirly.

"Where have you been, Anna? Where have you been?"

I didn't say anything cause it was a secret. I didn't say anything.

"Where have you been? Where have you been? Tell me! Tell me!" She was crying and shaking me. Shaking me hard. "Were you with your Grandpa John? Were you?"

I nodded my head. I was scared.

Then she hugged me. Hugged me close. Pressing my face against her soft droopy bosom. Rocking me, rocking me back and forth, back and forth. Crying, crying softly.

"Don't you ever go with your Grandpa John again. Do you hear me? Don't you ever go with him again." Stroking my hair, stroking my hair. "Come and get me. I won't let him, I won't let him hurt you . . . I'm sorry, child . . . I'm so sorry."

When she finally let me go, I went outside and lay on the lawn. Stared up at the sky, watched the clouds.

Didn't drink any soda. Kind of lost my taste for it.

Didn't tell anybody. I can keep a secret.

Wheat Germ

Mama had to get a job cause Daddy stopped working. He said painting all those highway patrol offices gave him a bum arm. So now he stays home all day. Stays home and eats wheat germ. Wheat germ and granola. Said it was for his arm, was gonna make it all better.

We waited and waited for his arm to get better. Kept bringing him bowls of wheat germ. But his arm didn't.

So now he doesn't go to work anymore. Just stays at home all day long. Smoking, reading and bossing us kids.

Then one day, he even stopped eating wheat germ. I'd gotten a bowl ready. With milk and honey. Just the way he liked it.

"Here's your wheat germ, Daddy," I said.

I thought he didn't hear me cause he didn't answer, so I said it again. "Daddy! Here's your wheat germ!"

"I don't want it," he said.

"Excuse me," I said. I thought maybe I'd heard him wrong. "Excuse me, Daddy, I didn't hear you."

"I said *I don't want it!*"

I realized I must have heard him right. But I still didn't know what to do. He was supposed to eat wheat germ and granola to make his arm better. And I'd fixed it up for him, just the way he liked it. Fixed it up with honey and milk. So I stayed there holding out the bowl.

He snapped his newspaper down. "What are you standing there for?" he demanded, glaring at me.

"I have your wheat germ, Daddy," I said in a small voice. "Your wheat germ to make your arm better."

The next thing I knew I had a bowl of wheat germ, honey and milk on my head. Not just on top, cause it glooped and dribbled and slopped down my face, neck, shoulders, even some on my shoes. School shoes!

I had to wash my hair and change my clothes and I was almost late for school.

It really hurt my feelings, but then I figured out why he did it. He did it because he decided he didn't want his arm to get better. He didn't want to go back to work. He just wanted to laze around the house all day and let Mama support the family.

And I never quite trusted this bum arm business anyway. I mean everyone else painted highway patrol offices and they didn't get bum arms! I painted a lot of highway patrol offices and my arms are just fine. As a matter of fact, I'm sure of it. He doesn't fool me. Not one little bit. I still offer him wheat germ. Offer it to him all the time. I just don't put milk and honey in it.

Turkey Dinner

There was a big storm. It snowed and snowed and snowed. Seemed like it would never end. They closed the schools and we stayed home and watched it snow. The sky was so dark, we had to keep the lights on even in the day. Dark and close. It snowed so hard that you couldn't see the woodshed from the kitchen door. So Mama let the boys sleep on the living room floor. She was scared they would miss the woodshed and keep on going and get lost and die.

Then one day, as quick as the snow started, it stopped. Just like that. And in the nick of time too, cause Grandmother was coming from Milwaukee for Thanksgiving and Mama and Daddy had to go to the airport to pick her up. They'd bought a big turkey and everything, cause Grandmother is real rich and used to eating good food all the time.

We don't see her very much cause she is so busy. She plays bridge and goes on cruise ships around the world. She has gold slippers and real gold jewelry, diamonds even! And she goes to the beauty parlor once every two weeks.

Once I got to stay at her house. Overnight too! Mama and I took the train. And for my bedtime story Grandmother told me how she ran away from home when she was fourteen. Her father didn't believe women needed an education. Well she wanted one. So she ran away to Illinois and put herself through school and college by being a live-in help with a family. Then she met Grandfather. Her friends thought he was a good catch, so she married him.

In the morning Grandmother made some oatmeal. She knows how to cook. I guess that's why Mama never learned. But when it came time to eat it, she didn't have any milk. Which I thought was strange, cause nobody eats oatmeal without milk. But she told me she was allergic to it. I thought she was teasing me, cause we just had Cool Whip on our Jell-O the evening before. So I mentioned it, and she said Cool Whip was an oil product, it just tasted like it was made out of milk. And then I said, "So if you wanted you could have Cool Whip on your oatmeal?" And she said, "Yes . . ." And so then I said, "Could I have Cool Whip on my oatmeal?" I was pretty sure she'd say no, cause Cool Whip is pretty expensive, and fancy too. But she just smiled and said, "I don't see why not." So I put Cool Whip on my oatmeal and it tasted real good. Grandmother thought it was funny to put Cool Whip on oatmeal. But I made her take a taste and she liked it so much that she put a spoonful on hers! And then when I got back home she wrote me a letter and told me that now every morning she puts Cool Whip in her oatmeal.

I wish I could have Cool Whip in my oatmeal every morning. Actually I don't. It's kind of a waste of good Cool Whip. I'd rather just eat it plain.

Anyway, we had this huge turkey in the fridge waiting for the big day. Sweet potatoes too! Just thinking about it was enough to make my mouth water. Lots and lots of food! As much as you wanted! Second helpings! Thirds!

So we were glad when the snow let up. Mama and Daddy went to the airport. Me and Susan made the stuffing, while Joy washed the turkey, inside and out, in case of leftover guts. Katie scrubbed the sweet potatoes. We made a good stuffing. With old stale bread, celery, onions, margarine, and spice. Tasted good. We checked before we stuffed the turkey just to make sure. Then we popped it in the oven at three hundred and twenty-five degrees and made a baste of red wine and melted margarine. We didn't have a basting brush, so we found an old yellow toothbrush that nobody was using and used that instead. Washed it out good though. Soap and water so there wouldn't be any germs. Basted the turkey, and went outside to play.

The snow was deep! Real deep! Over four feet in places! Tons and tons of snow. We had snowball fights, made forts, a snowman, angels. It was fun. Then Susan had a great idea . . . a slide! *A giant slide!*

See, the roof of this house was made out of aluminum sheet metal. You know, the kind they use on barns.

So what we did was jump out of the upstairs window, slide down the roof, fast, real fast, then you'd go soaring out into the air and for a few seconds you really felt like you were flying. It was scary. Real scary, like at any second you could die, and then *blam!* You'd land in the soft snow.

It was a good thing Mama wasn't home, cause it might have made her feel a little nervous.

We slid down the roof all afternoon. We only stopped to baste the turkey and put the sweet potatoes in the oven.

Abby Road was real curious. Kept trying to get upstairs, see what all the fun was . . . But we didn't let her. Didn't want her to get hurt.

But when Grandmother came, in all the excitement, someone must have forgotten to shut the upstairs door.

Cause when Grandmother stepped on the front porch in all her fancy Milwaukee clothes . . .

There was a thump, whiz-bang! And the next thing you know, Abby Road went sailing over our heads and landed headfirst in the snow!

Grandmother was screaming, "What's that? What's that thing?" Hugging her coat tight around her. And poor Abby Road was stuck but good. Her four legs were waving around and kicking like crazy!

We ran out in the snow and pulled her out. Didn't even put our boots on. Didn't want her to suffocate! We were laughing cause it was funny, but Mama was not impressed!

When we got inside we showed Grandmother all of our fancy cooking. How we remembered to baste the turkey so it would be nice and juicy, but she didn't seem to be too excited. Said it looked very good, but she was on a diet. Didn't eat any turkey. Only took half a sweet potato. Didn't eat it though. Just mashed it around on her plate.

I ate! I ate *a lot!* I was real hungry from all that playing. And it was the best turkey dinner I'd ever had.

Three

My Room!

We've moved again. To Diamond Lake this time. Outside of Diamond Lake actually, forty-five minutes. But I like to say we live in Diamond Lake cause it's such a pretty name. It's a big ranch house and we get to stay for free. All we have to do is fix up the little white house down the road. And Daddy can do that even with a bum arm. But the best thing of all is, I have my own room! See, there were three bedrooms. One for Mama and Daddy. One for Nick, Matthew and Jimmie. And one for us girls. But when I was exploring, I found, in the very back of the basement, a little door. It had a key in the lock, one of those old-fashioned keys. I turned it. The door opened, and . . . inside was the sweetest little room. With shelves, lots of shelves, lining the walls, top to bottom. Just perfect for me to put all my clothes, books, marbles and things. I'm a good marble shooter. At my old school I started off with one cat-eye that I found in an old dust pile of garbage and leaves. One little old cat-eye and by the time we moved I could barely tie them all up in my fine lady scarf. Pee-wees, cleary boulders, cat-eyes, everything. I'd loop my scarf around the belt loop on my pants and they'd rumble when I walked. Got so when kids saw me coming, they'd scoop up their marbles and say they'd just closed for the day. I'd pretend to argue, say they weren't playing fair, but deep inside I was proud. Felt like a character out of the Wild West.

So anyway, I didn't tell anybody about this room I'd found, just ran straight upstairs and asked Mama if I could have it. She looked kind of confused so I grabbed her hand and dragged her downstairs to see. First she said no because my bed wouldn't fit in, but I told her I didn't like sleeping on my bed anymore, I liked the floor better! And then she said, "But concrete, Anna. It's pretty hard." So I lay down and showed her that it wasn't, and it wasn't hard! It was really quite soft! So finally she smiled and said okay, but in the winter I'd have to come upstairs and share with my sisters again.

I ran upstairs to pack as fast as I could before one of my sisters found out and raised a big ruckus and got it instead of me.

Unfortunately, Susan was in our room reading. So I couldn't pack quite as fast as I wanted to. Had to do it nonchalant-like, so I wouldn't draw attention to myself. Pick up a few things out of my drawer. Hold them up to me like I was trying to decide what to wear to the new school, then put them down on my spread-out blanket. Pick up something else. All was going fine, real smooth until Katie came in the room.

"What are you doing, Anna? What are you doing?" I pretended not to hear her. But it didn't work, she just spoke louder. *"What are you doing, Anna? Huh? What are you doing?"* "Nothing," I said under my breath. "Go away." *"No!"* she yelled in her supersonic voice. *"No! I won't go away! It's my room too!"* I could see that my packing time was rapidly drawing to a close. Susan looked up. "What are you doing, Anna?" she asked. "Nothing!" I said in a loud voice. "Just leave me alone!" By now all pretense of trying on school clothes was gone. I was just pulling my clothes out of the drawer like crazy, and flinging them on my blanket. Then I grabbed my fancy lady scarf off the wall, threw it on the top of my heap of stuff, snatched up the corners of my blanket, and heaved it over my shoulder and marched out of the room.

"Anna's running away!" squealed Katie at the top of her lungs. *"Anna's running away!"* Well I started running, but it didn't do any good, cause she started running after me screaming, *"Anna's running away! Anna's running awaaaaay!"*

By the time I got to the basement practically everyone was thundering after me. Matthew, Susan, Nick, Jimmie, Katie, Joy. I ran as fast as I could to the door, opened it, leapt inside, slammed it shut and leaned against it, hot, scared. I could hear the rumble of their voices outside the door, Katie's high-pitched squeak, and Jimmie crying, "Don't run away, Anna . . . don't run away!" I waited for them to leave, but they didn't.

I put my stuff down, opened the door a crack and

peered through. Not a big crack, just a tiny one, as narrow as a pencil. I could see colors, legs, arms, bodies, moving, jostling about. So I yelled through the crack, I yelled as loud as I could. *"Go away!"* And then slammed the door shut again. But they didn't go away. I could hear them laughing. Laughing at me. Except for Jimmie, he was crying. So I flung the door open and glared at them. Glared at them and smiled at Jimmie so he'd know I was okay. Behind them I could see a trail of clothes that had escaped from my blanket. I wanted to get them, but I didn't dare leave my room cause someone else would dart in and then it would be theirs. Just in case someone tried, I stretched my arms and legs out across the doorway to make a big X.

There was a pause while everyone stared at me. Then Susan said, "Anna, what are you doing?"

I tightened my arms and legs even harder. I could feel my face was red and stubborn.

"It's mine!" I said, loudly. They just looked at me so I said it again louder. *"It's mine! Mama said so! It's mine!"*

"What's yours? What are you talking about?"

"It's *mine! My room!*"

"What room?" Susan bent over and picked Jimmie up.

"This room, this is *my room!* You can't have it. It's *mine!* Mama said so." And I don't know why, but I started to cry.

Susan edged forward, Jimmie slung on her hip, and peered over the shoulder of my X.

"What is it? What is it?" squeaked Katie. But Susan didn't answer. She just looked over my shoulder at my room. She looked and she looked, then she kind of cleared her throat, turned around and started towards the basement stairs. Walked right by everyone, kind of stiff and quiet.

When she got to the stairs she didn't turn around, just said in a kind of strange voice, "I didn't want it anyway." And then she walked real stiff-backed up the stairs, taking Jimmie with her.

When they left it was like a spell was broken. Nick, Matthew and Joy pushed past me and tromped around my room laughing. "You call this a *room? Ha ha ha!* It's a cupboard, or a pantry or something! *Ha ha ha!*" And then they left. So the only problem I had was Katie. She said she wanted it, and I said she couldn't, and then she said she was going to ask Mama, and I told her if she did I'd punch her on the arm and hard too. And she said she'd tell and I said I didn't care, and then she started towards my room and so I put up my fists and so she left, cause she knew I meant it.

The Thief

Daddy was supposed to go back to our old home and get Abby Road. Abby Road and Mama's baby grand piano cause they wouldn't fit in the first truckload.

Well, someone stole Mama's baby grand, cause when Daddy went to pick it up, it was gone! And Abby Road was gone too! And when Daddy came back and told Mama, she cried and cried, saying, "My daddy gave me that . . . my daddy gave me that . . ."

Well Daddy got real mad. Yelled and yelled. Said Mama was being selfish. That it was just a stupid piano! Ridiculous that a family in our position would even contemplate keeping such an expensive toy! But Mama just kept on crying, "My daddy bought me that . . . It was mine . . . mine!" And locked herself in the bedroom.

Daddy banged on the door. Banged hard, but Mama wouldn't open it. So he yelled, "Well your daddy's dead! So what cha gonna do now!"

Mama stayed in bed for three days. Only came out to eat and go to the bathroom. Didn't talk to Daddy.

She didn't seem to care that Abby Road was lost. Didn't even mention it.

Nick says Daddy killed her, and that's what we're eating now. But I don't believe him. He's just trying to bug me. I think another family has adopted her. A rich family. And she can have as much milk and as many Life Savers as she wants! I hope so.

But just in case, I've marked all the new packages of venison with a red X so if Nick is right, I won't eat her by accident.

Jimmie

Jimmie's gone. His mama showed up, wearing a cream-colored suit and her hair cut short and nylons. I didn't even recognize her.

"Hello," she says, looking kind of nervous. "I've come for my boy."

"Excuse me?" I say. Cause I'm not sure who she is, just have a kind of familiar feeling in my ribs. She looks over her shoulder at the man waiting for her in a cream-colored car that matches her suit, and says again, "My boy, I've come for my boy." I'm still not sure what she's talking about, but I notice she's got red shiny nail polish on.

"It's me, Mona," she says. Her shoes are cream-colored too, just like her suit and car.

"Is Jimmie here?"

I nod my head cause my voice is surprised, and I go to get him. But then I hear Daddy call, "Who's that? Who's that at the door?"

"Mona," I say. "She's come for Jimmie!"

Well Jimmie comes running. And Daddy comes running. And Mona's got her arms stretched out to Jimmie and she's crying, and Jimmie recognizes her right away. Which is pretty remarkable, since I didn't recognize her and I'm a lot older than he is, and he hasn't seen her for over a year. But he does. And he calls out, "Mommy!" and he almost gets to her, but Daddy gets there first. And he grabs Jimmie by the arm and says to Mona, "You can't have him. He's ours now!" And slams the door in her face.

Well Mona took Mama and Daddy to court. And she won, so Jimmie went to live with her. And I miss him, but I'm kind of glad too. Cause every time I saw him, I felt kind of guilty about the pooh.

Bird Lady

Mama and Daddy have taken on a boarder. The grade five, six and seven teacher. At school we're supposed to call him Mr. Coleman, but at home we call him Abe. Abe is short for Abraham, which is his real name.

He is tall, real tall, and has sandy hair, watery blue eyes and wire-rimmed glasses perched on his large bulbous red nose. It's rather amazing really, because it doesn't matter what the weather's like, hot or cold, it makes no difference to the redness of his nose. It's always red. When it gets really cold little purple veins stand out a little bit more, but that's about it. It never goes to the color of a normal person's nose. Anyway, except for his nose he's okay. And quite friendly to us kids, so I don't mind. The boys do though. They finally had a real bedroom, in the house, and then Mama and Daddy took on this boarder, and out the boys went to the barn. Which isn't a great place to live. It's fine in the day, but at night it's dark and spooky. With mice and spiders and rats and barn owls hooting in and out and flapping in your face. So needless to say, the boys aren't too crazy about Abe. And to make matters worse he's gonna be their teacher at school, so they'll never get a break from him.

Whenever he's out of earshot they call him Able-to-Do-Nothing and Ol' Potato Nose.

Anyway, the good thing about Abe staying in the boys' room, and the boys staying in the barn, is that I got to be a bird lady! I was a bird lady before, but not a real one, cause the only birds I could catch were the ones I saved from the cats. I managed to save quite a few, but they always died after a day or two cause of the fright and teeth marks. I had one bird that lasted for four days, but it died too. And I was real sad so Nick found the barn owl's nest and when she was out, he climbed up the rafters and stole one of its babies for me, and I loved it so much that he stole me another one! "An early birthday present!" he said. So I had two baby barn owls! Real ones! And they were *alive!*

Katie and Joy were real envious until they saw how much work they were. Cause baby barn owls eat *a lot!* And I had to catch it. Once they ate thirty-eight grasshoppers in *one day!* I wasn't sure what I was going to do once school started, cause when they were hungry it took me all day to catch enough food.

They pooped a lot too. So it probably was a good thing I had my room in the basement, cause all that pooh was making my room a little stinky. But I didn't mind. The smell didn't bother me. I think probably cause I'm part bird. The reason I know this is because I kind of understand their language. I knew when they were hungry or thirsty or scared. And they thought I was their mama. When I went for walks, I'd put one on each shoulder and they'd dig their little claws in and wind their tiny beaks around and around in my hair so they wouldn't fall off. And I'd have to walk real straight and smooth and slow, with my hands cupped up close so I could catch them in case they fell.

I loved having those pet owls. I had them for three and a half whole weeks, but then one day the door to my room wasn't shut properly and the cat got in and ate one. And then the other one wouldn't eat any food or water for four days, and then finally died of a broken heart.

I cried and cried.

Nick tried to make it up to me. Helped me catch a pet skunk. We were out looking for the cow when I saw it. Nick said, "Noooooo way! I'm not helping nobody catch a skunk!" But he did. We chased it and chased it until it got too tired to run anymore, and then we threw my jacket on it, wrapped it up and snuck it into my room. It was real nice. Liked me too. Real tame, didn't bite me or stink me or anything. Made a real good pet. I just fed it raw eggs and water. But then one day Mama came downstairs before I had a chance to hide it, and she got kind of upset and made me take it outside, "Far, far, *far* away from the house . . ." and let it go.

My Grade

Mama skipped Katie! Mama skipped her cause in the new school Mama's the grade three, four and five teacher. Well I'm in grade three, Joy's in grade four, and Susan is in grade five. And Mama felt it wasn't fair for Katie to be left out. Why? I don't know! It's not like it's a birthday party or anything. We're just in Mama's class. And Katie should be in Mrs. Norman's class. "We'll just let her try it and see how she likes it." But what about me? What about how I like it!

Needless to say, Katie loves it. So now not only are her feet bigger than mine, but she's in my grade too!

It really gets me. Now that she's in my grade she thinks she's superior to me. And she's not polite at all. She just doesn't know how people do things in my grade. She never waits until other people figure out the answer. No sir. The very second a question is out of Mama's mouth, up springs Katie's hand. Shooting up with such force you think she's going to propel herself straight through the ceiling. And if she says some stupid answer and people laugh, she doesn't care. Up shoots her hand again on the very next question.

And she is in the spelling group above me! *Above me!* I can't take it! I really can't! Every time the spelling groups are called out, she turns around and smirks at me. Smirks and then saunters off to her group.

And then cause she's littler she never has anyone to eat lunch with or play with. I mean of course! She's a baby! Who's gonna want to eat lunch with her? And she makes herself so obnoxious, what does she expect? You can't spend your day making people feel stupid and then expect them to want to eat lunch with you.

So she sits there with her chin jutting out, acting like she doesn't care. And what am I supposed to do? Not eat lunch with my friends? Play with her all recess? What am I supposed to do?

When I play with her, I treat her real mean. And when I play with my friends, my stomach hurts.

Susan and Joy think it's funny. Katie being in my grade. They think it's cute. But they don't have to deal with it. They don't have to eat lunch with her. They just go off with their friends! Off with their friends and leave me to cope.

Wrigley's Spearmint Gum

Mama, Abe and I were in town shopping. Mama had to get something from the drugstore, and it was taking a while, so I went to look at the candy section.

Abe was already there looking at the gum. Wrigley's spearmint gum. A big package of it. A big package with lots of little packages inside. Little packages all lined up.

I was just about to say, "Hi, Abe!" when he opened up his old brown coat and slipped the gum inside. Sliding it smooth against his warm checked shirt. Red and navy flannel. Crossing his arms casual, didn't want it to slip, straightening his body, glancing around, making sure no one saw him. And no one did see him. No one but me.

He looked at me for a moment. Looked at me over the top of his glasses with a guilty half smile. Then he winked and tapped his finger to his lips.

"Hi, kid!" he said in a loud jolly voice. "Where's your mom?"

"She's getting medicine," I said, looking at him, feeling kind of confused.

"Well . . . Let's go find her."

So we found her. She was right where I left her.

She paid for her medicine and we started to go.

I watched him and watched him, but he didn't pay. Just walked right out. Smiling at everyone. "How do you do?" and "Good day." Stolen gum pressed up against his belly.

When we got in the car, he turned around in his seat and ruffled my hair. "You did great!" he said.

"What?" Mama asked. "What are you talking about?"

But he just smiled. "Oh nothing," he said, and winked at me again.

He tried to slip me a pack of gum. One little piddly pack. Like that was going to buy me off, when he had stolen a whole bunch. Maybe fifty or a hundred! I shook my head and glared at him from under my bangs. Wouldn't take it. He tried to put it in my hand, but I put my hands behind my back. So finally he put it on the seat beside me.

When we got home, I just got out of the car. Head high. And marched into the house. Left it on the seat.

But I couldn't stop thinking about that gum. Gum sitting on the seat waiting for me. I knew that if I didn't eat it someone else would. So I went back and I got it.

Katie and I met in the barn, and I told her about it. We decided to chew it. It tasted good. We decided we wanted some more. So we snuck into Abe's room and found where he hid the gum and stole some more.

After all what could he say? "Somebody stole some of the gum I stole"?

Changes

I'm not quite sure what happened at school but something definitely happened. First of all, Abe left. One day he was there teaching, and the next day he wasn't. Moved out of the boys' room too.

Gone. Just like that.

And Mama crying. Crying all the time. And Daddy yelling and then crying and then yelling some more.

And the boys have a new teacher. Mr. Frew. But

Mama pulled them out of school cause she didn't trust him. "He's a Boy Scout leader," says Mama real pointedly. "And we all know why he does that . . ."

I don't know why, but it must be something bad.

And then at school all of a sudden, none of the kids liked Mama anymore. Which is strange, cause they all used to. And nobody would play with us. Play with us or talk to us. No one but Randy. And I don't want to talk to him, cause he was my boyfriend for three days. He kept saying he was going to marry me. He gave me a golden ring. Real gold. I wore it for a little while, but it gave my finger claustrophobia, and made my stomach hurt. So I gave it back and told him I didn't want to be his girlfriend anymore. Didn't think anything of it. Everybody's always breaking up, no problem. But he got really upset. His face got real pale, slightly greenish blue around the eyes, nose and mouth. Like he needed to throw up or something. And me, just standing there holding out that gold ring.

Then he lunged at me. I thought he was going to hit me, but he didn't. He grabbed the ring and threw it. He threw it real far. Way up over the school fence.

I was kind of surprised, cause I had no idea he was such a good thrower. And then he started crying. Crying and half running, half stumbling across the field. When he got to the other end he turned around and yelled, "I'm never gonna have another girlfriend as long as I live!" Yelled it as loud as he could for the whole world to hear. Quiet little Randy who never talked! Then he ran right out of the schoolyard. Which is one of the number one school rules. "Don't leave the school grounds without permission." But he did. Left the school grounds and didn't come back for the rest of the day.

My sisters thought it was romantic. But I didn't. It just hurts my stomach every time I think about it.

Anyway, nobody would talk to us, so finally I cornered Peggy Doyle.

"What's going on?" I said, grabbing hold of her arm.

"Let go of me!" she said, trying to get by. But I wouldn't.

"Why won't you talk to me? Why won't you play with me anymore?"

"Because . . ."

"Because why?"

"Because . . ." Then all of a sudden she got real defiant and pushed me, pushed me hard.

"Because your mama's a hoor!"

I wasn't sure what that meant, but I knew it wasn't nice. So I said, "Is not!" And pushed her back and so she said, "Is too!" And pushed me back. And then more kids joined in and then my sisters joined in and pretty soon it seemed like we were up against the whole school. The whole school except Randy. He was fighting with us.

So Mama quit school, and pulled us girls from school. She said she'd teach us at home. But she never quite gets around to it. Just lies in bed all day. Lies in bed and cries.

Island

We're moving again. To an island! One of the little San Juan islands in Washington State. I've never lived on an island before! But it's supposed to be wonderful! With Indians and leprechauns and things!

Now you might think that there are only leprechauns in Ireland . . . But when Mama was looking at our new house . . . Just out of the corner of her eye, she saw a flash of green. When she went over to see what it was, she found a whole bunch of chocolate bars in the shape of a four-leaf clover! And as she was looking at it in amazement, she heard this little chuckling. Real quiet. But she has real good ears so she heard it, and so she kept her whole body real still, and just turned her eyes to look. Not even blinking, turned her eyes to where the chuckling was coming from . . . and she saw him . . . the leprechaun! He was around as tall as her thumb, not counting her fingernail, and he was dressed all in green, and had a red beard and red hair, and twinkling eyes. She only saw him for a second though, cause she blinked and when she opened her eyes again he was gone. And she thought maybe it was a dream, except when she looked down, there were the chocolate bars. Chocolate bars with sparkling green leprechaun magic on them. And I know this is true cause she brought them home and we ate them! So Mama knew right then, that this was a sign, a sign that this island was the place for us.

So she decided to buy the house rather than rent it. And it sounds just perfect. Apple trees, cherry trees, pear trees, a creek! So little they don't even have a policeman or a proper grocery store. You have to take a *ferry boat* to the mainland to get your groceries!

So anyway we just have to wait until our mortgage comes through and then we're moving. Settling down for good! And it shouldn't take too long, cause Mama said they need teachers out there something fierce.

Strawberry Pickers

On our way up to Washington, Daddy decided to visit Grandma Marge. She's his mom.

Mama wasn't too pleased about the idea. She's never really liked Grandma Marge ever since she gave Mama a year's subscription to *Good Housekeeping* for a Christmas present. Mama got real offended. Thought it was a hint or something. And when I finally met Grandma Marge, I realized Mama was probably right.

She's the kind of person who always makes you feel like you've done something wrong, you're dirty or something. Like the very sight of you is distasteful, but she'll tolerate it. She's not soft and comforting like normal grandmothers. She's tough and stringy like beef jerky. White hair. White, white hair. Not a speck of gray in it, and false teeth that clack when she chews. She smells of mothballs. Mothballs and old sweaters.

And she makes you drink all the juice from the canned peaches. Choke it down while she sits in her armchair, clicking her knitting needles. Never taking her eyes off you until you've swallowed every last drop. Then she'd say, "Upstairs. Get ready for bed." And we'd look at Mama, cause our bedtime wasn't for another two hours. But Mama'd just sit there on the sofa. Hands limp, pretending not to notice.

"Hop to it!" Grandma Marge would say, clapping her hands twice. So we'd hop to it and get into bed, and lie there forever, bodies twisting and turning. Waiting for night.

No talking, no stories, or up she'd come. Up the stairs to glare at us with her ice cube eyes. Glare at us and complain to Mama and Daddy how bad we are.

Then one morning she came downstairs and said she had figured it out. What us kids needed was to be kept busy. Kept out of trouble. A neighbor of hers had a strawberry field that needed picking, and she told him we'd help. He'd pay us ten cents a flat. "But no eating!" she said. "Don't embarrass me," she said. "Don't want him to think I don't feed you proper."

The next morning she crammed us full of gooey eggs and cold toast. Watching like an eagle that we ate every bite. Then she plopped old straw hats on our heads and marched us down the road. One mile and a half, to her neighbors' house.

Mr. and Mrs. Kimble gave us the flats and showed us how to pick. We picked and picked and picked. Kneeling down in the hot dry dirt. Sun beating down on our backs. Hot, hot sun. Arms, shoulders, necks sore, aching. Knees tired of kneeling. Picking and picking, not wanting to embarrass the family. Mouths dry, thirsty. Thirsty for the ripe red berries. Sneaking a few, only a few. Quietly, quickly, pretending to cough. Hastily wiping with the back of a dusty dirty hand. Wiping away the traces. The traces of weakness. Grandma Marge carefully checking our faces when we dragged our bodies home.

"No way to spend a vacation . . ." we'd whisper. "No way to spend the holidays . . ."

Finally the strawberry season was over.

The Kimbles had a party. A party for all the pickers. So after dinner Susan, Joy and Katie and me washed our faces and got dressed in our good clothes. Nick and Matthew said they weren't coming. Seen enough of that stinking old field. But I guess all our hustle-bustle and excitement must have rubbed off, cause when it was time to go, there they were. Hair plastered down with water. It seemed funny walking down to the Kimbles' in the evening. Light dusky summer evening. The frogs and crickets just starting to wake up. Excited. Real excited. We got to stay up late, and it was rumored that we'd get to eat as many strawberries as we liked! And we were going to eat mountains! Mountains and mountains!

And we did. And they were good.

There was a teenage boy there. He won the prize for the best picker. Five dollars! He said "Thanks" and shoved it in his back pocket. Then he grabbed a big handful of strawberries, ripe juicy ones, and started chasing this girl. She had wavy blond hair, down to her shoulders. He grabbed her and wrestled her to the ground. Rolling and rolling in the dirt. Laughing. Laughing and screaming and then laughing again. Smearing strawberries. Strawberries all over. In her hair, her face, her mouth. Strawberries. Strawberries ruining her white summer blouse.

Then all of a sudden they became quiet. Just looked at each other. Breathing hard.

He flipped himself over so he was lying on top of her, and they kissed. A long kiss. When they finished he lifted his head up and looked at her. And she looked at him, like the whole world had stopped, just them. His hand came up and smoothed her strawberry-smeared hair out of her eyes. She smiled and he got up. Dusted off his pants, then gave her his hand and helped her up. Gentle, so gentle. He dusted her off. And they walked away. Walked away before the party was over. Holding hands, him whistling softly. Walked away into the golden dusty night.

Forever House

Our new home is two stories high. Three if you count the basement. And it has four bedrooms! Three upstairs and one downstairs.

To start out with Mama and Daddy got the big bedroom downstairs. Nick and Matthew had one of the big ones upstairs. Joy and Susan had the other one. And Katie and I shared the little one. But then Nick and Matthew decided they didn't want a bedroom. Funny after all their bellyaching about never getting one. But they didn't like Mama and Daddy always yelling up the stairs to be quiet, and early bedtimes and everything. So they decided to sleep in the big old green truck we bought to move everything up here. And since Mama and Daddy had no problem with the boys taking over the truck, out they went. And now Nick and Matthew strut around like the cocks of the walk. "No one telling us what to do." Swagger . . . swagger . . . "No sissy bedtimes for us, we just sneak out whenever we like! Stay awake as late as we like!" Like they're oh so special. But I don't care. Now I get my own room. We all do, cause Joy moved into the boys' old room. And then Katie got jealous, cause she wanted her own bedroom. So she moved into the closet across the hall. Said it was just the right size for her. Slept on the top shelf that was for hats or sweaters or something. Made it cozy with all her stuffed animals. And since Katie moved out of our room it left me with my own room again!

And the outside of our house is real pretty. It's white, with a blue roof and sky-blue window frames. And there really are fruit trees, and huckleberry bushes, and wild strawberries and blackberries. And there is a creek. Our creek, on our property! And someday we're going to buy chickens and ducks and a cow maybe. And have a garden and grow our own food and everything. Not only that, there are wild mushrooms. Daddy got real excited when he found out. Took the ferry to the mainland and bought a book on mushrooms. Taught us all about them, which ones are edible and so on. There is one mushroom in particular that we have to look out for. It is poisonous and if we were to see it we must bring it home to Daddy so he can get rid of it, cause he doesn't want any accidents happening.

I've found lots of good ones, puffballs and the ones that look like brown lace umbrellas. But I've never found one of those mushrooms Daddy keeps asking about. The poisonous ones.

I love our new house. And I think the thing I love about it the most is that we don't have to move anymore. We're staying here forever. The forever house.

Fine Ladies, Katie, Daddy and the Raspberries

When Daddy decides to spank somebody, he's going to spank somebody. It doesn't matter who you are, or even if you've done something wrong. If he feels like spanking, and you're there, he'll spank you and then find a reason. So the trick is to be out of the room when Daddy's in a spanking mood. And if you can't get out of the room in time, then hide. In cupboards, under the sofa, behind the fridge was the best place. He never looked there.

It was still summer, so we hadn't started at our new school yet, but we were doing learning of another sort. Susan was giving us "fine lady" lessons.

We had just practiced the eating section at breakfast. We learned that fine ladies delicately suck the tip of every finger after every bite, making a dainty little smack. Then you wiggle your fingers slightly to dry them, and say in a cultured fine lady voice, "Ah . . . deeelicious." We also learned that fine ladies always leave a bit of food on their plate. The more fine they are the more of their food they leave. This was the hardest part for us. We were always hungry.

I had managed to leave the most. Not just one little dab of one thing. No sir. I left a dab of everything on my plate! A quarter of a piece of toast. A tablespoon of my scrambled eggs. And the biggest sacrifice of all, I didn't eat my eighth of a cantaloupe down to the dark green rind. I only ate it to the pale green with a little orange around the edge! We didn't get cantaloupe very often. Since I had accomplished this feat, much to the amazement of my sisters, I was certain I would indeed be a fine lady when I grew up. Another thing I was certain of was that Joy never would be. Half the time she forgot to smack her fingers. When she did remember, she'd stick them in her mouth all the way to her second knuckle and then pull them out with a loud popping slurping noise. Not daintily like me. She ate all of her food on her plate except one little crust of bread. And when we left to go upstairs for our fainting lesson, I saw her grab her crust and stuff it in her mouth. But even worse. She started grabbing the food off my plate too! The outrage! I was hungry too! But I left that food so people would think I was a fine lady. And now there she was gobbling it up, not even leaving a trace!

"That's my food! That's mine!" I shrieked. "How dare you eat my fine lady scraps!"

Joy looked up. Mouth trapped in mid-chew.

"How dare you eat my food!" I screamed, cultured fine lady voice gone.

Susan floated down the stairs. "Ladies, ladies, what is all this ruckus? Fine ladies do not shriek, Anna, they speak in cool modulated tones."

"Joy ate my food!" I bellowed with righteous indignation. Katie peeked out from behind Susan curiously.

Joy seemed to get shorter. "I was hungry," she mumbled. Mouth still full of unchewed guilty evidence.

"So . . . was . . . I!" I stated loudly. It was worth the food. To have such an audience, when I was so undeniably right.

Just then Daddy's bedroom door flew open, and Daddy burst through. Naked as usual. Face red, penis flapping. He was in a spanking mood. Needless to say we all ran away and hid. All that is but Katie, she tripped over her fine lady petticoat and fell flat on her face. Daddy grabbed her arm. And it wasn't to help her up either. Well he did help her up, but that was only so he could spank her. *Spank! Spank!* "I told you to keep . . ." *Spank!* "it down . . ." *Spank!* "in the morning!" *Spank!* "Goddamned stupid . . ." *Spank!* "kids . . ." *Spank!* "Spoiled! Rotten!" *Spank!* "Kids!" *Spank!* "Ungrateful little brats!" *Spank! Spank! Spank!* Then he stomped back into his bedroom.

Daddy's favorite fruit was raspberries. Now Katie just happened to know where a wild raspberry bush was. It was a long way away. Close to two miles. Hard to get at. And that spanking must have left Katie in no walking mood. But she marched out of the kitchen and straight to that raspberry bush. Dress-up clothes and all.

When she came back, we were playing outside. Her dress-up petticoat was torn and dirty. Right hand clenched in a fist. Face grubby and smeared.

"Where's Daddy?" she demanded.

"Inside," Susan answered.

"Come on." She marched inside, and we followed, close behind.

Daddy was in the living room reading a book in his black vinyl chair.

When we were all in the living room, she said in a loud voice to no one in particular, "Look what I have." She opened her hand. Inside were eight slightly mushed raspberries.

"Raspberries!" she said. "Um . . . yum!" Then she came over to us and popped one into each of our mouths, saying, "One for you, Anna, cause I like you . . . And one for you, Susan, cause I like you . . . And one for you, Joy, cause I like you . . ." And so on, until she had given everyone in the room one but Daddy. Then she walked over to Daddy. We all watched. She stood in front of him. He smiled expectantly. As I said before, raspberries were Daddy's favorite fruit.

"And . . ." she said, slowly picking up the last raspberry out of the palm of her grubby little hand. She paused for a second. Then she bellowed "None for you! Cause you're mean to me and I *don't* like you!" And she popped that last raspberry in her mouth and ate it! Well Daddy gave her another spanking even harder. *Spank! Spank!*

Spank! The strange thing is Katie didn't even cry. She just stood there with a triumphant look on her face. The more he spanked, the happier she looked. I don't know how anybody could be happy about a spanking.

French Fries

We were playing restaurant. I personally would have rather played nightclub. But we didn't have any money and you need money for the cherries. Maraschino cherries. They're quite expensive. We like red ones best, beautiful ruby red ones. Sometimes they'd be out of red, and then we'd buy green. They didn't taste quite as good though, and there's something about all that redness that feels more like a nightclub. Sophisticated and stuff. Anyway, we'd get a bottle of maraschino cherries, and then dress in our finest nightclub clothes, slinky and sexy, with perfumed lipstick and blue mascara. And Susan would put on purple eyeshadow on account of her eyes. How she got purple eyes I don't know, as the rest of us kids just have plain old brown. We'd brush our hair a hundred strokes so it would be soft and silky. Sometimes we'd wrap it in rags the night before so it would be curly like a movie star. Then when we were all ready, we would drift downstairs to the kitchen and arrange the chairs in a semi-circle around the table.

Mix and mingle, polite conversation about trips abroad, our trouble with the servants, the cost of our fancy diamonds, emeralds, sapphires. Conversation punctuated with sighs, faints, and wafting arms.

Then one of us, usually Susan, would flash the kitchen lights. *Flash! Flash!* On and off! On and off! On and off! Just like a nightclub, and wrap the other hand around the mouth to make a trumpet. First finger and thumb making an O shape and the other three wiggling up and down. A loud booming voice that would send shivers of excitement along our spines. *"And now, ladies and gentlemen! The show is about to begin! Ta da ta daaaa!"* Then she'd really flash those lights. If we'd managed to get the grown-ups to watch, they'd clap, and we'd get in line. But more often than not the grown-ups were too busy or tired or grouchy. And if that was the case, then we'd just clap good and loud, and cheer, and I'd pretend to do wolf whistles. I can do a pretty good imitation using my voice and I figure with the lights out, who's going to know the difference. Then when we were all in line, the announcer would say in her announcer voice, *"And now, ladies and gentlemen, I bring you the leopards!"* A frenzy of flashing now for emphasis, then the announcer would leave the lights on, dart into line, and the show would begin!

We'd smile, nod graciously and blow kisses in the direction of the kitchen table, and grab our mikes. The salt and pepper shakers are the best cause they are longer than the spice jars and a better shape, but any spice jar will do really. And then we'd sing our opening song. Susan wrote it. It's called "The Leopards." It goes like this. "Here we are the leopards, the leopards again, we come from the jungle across the mighty plains, here we are all gathered together to sing you a song by *the Leopards!*" At this point Katie and I, who are on the ends of the line, fall onto our knees and spread our arms out in front of us at shoulder level, and Susan and Joy stay standing and turn cheek to cheek and put their arms out at waist level. Katie and I have the tough part of it cause at the point we have to fall down on our knees the song goes up very high and it's kind of hard to sing up high when you're falling down low, so we both tend to squeak on that part. Not to mention bruising our knees. Anyway that's really the only difficult part of the evening, after that it's just sit back and enjoy.

We take turns singing and being the audience. Both are fun. Singing cause everyone is looking at you, and we're all pretty good singers, except Katie. She's not a very good singer, she sings loud and off key. I'm the best singer actually. Susan and Joy can sing on key but not very loud. But I can sing loud and on key. So I'm the best singer.

We sing solos and duets and when we start running out of radio songs, we sing Christmas songs. We know lots of Christmas songs, harmonies and everything.

The problem we used to have with nightclub, was that everyone wanted to sing and no one wanted to be the audience. That's how we came up with the idea of the cocktails! We'd mix up a bit of sugar water, add a drop of food coloring, whatever color you wanted, and then plop in a maraschino cherry. It looks real pretty, and tastes good too! And after singing for a while, you get mighty thirsty and tired, so a nice comfortable chair and a delicious drink hits the spot.

So even though nightclub is my favorite, it's not what we were doing now. For one thing, you can't really play nightclub in broad daylight, cause then it wouldn't be nightclub, it would be dayclub. And dayclub just doesn't have the same ring. Besides, you could flash the lights all you want, but nobody would notice, and even if they did, it wouldn't be very dramatic if you know what I mean. You'd feel kinda foolish. And we'd probably get in trouble for having the lights on during the day and wasting electricity. So we were playing restaurant instead.

It was Joy's turn to be restaurant owner.

Susan, Katie and I sat in our fine lady clothes around the card table under the king apple tree. She'd decorated the table up real nice. Put her blanket over it just like a tablecloth. Normally, I wouldn't fancy eating off of Joy's blanket cause she pees the bed. But because we were outdoors, you could hardly smell it, and she'd found some wildflowers and stuck them in an empty mayonnaise jar, and it looked real pretty.

As we were taking our seats a wasp flew up and landed on the tablecloth, which caused a moment of panic, but I guess it could smell the pee better than us, cause it left again in a real hurry.

Then Joy came loping out of the house, wiping her big red-knuckled hands on her apron, a red and white polka-dot shirt tied around her waist.

"Hello, fancy ladies!" she said, beaming. "And how may I help you?" She had a tall chef's hat she made out of newspaper on her head.

We only looked at her out of the corners of our eyes. Noses in the air, pretending not to notice her.

"Excuse me, fancy ladies," she said again, trying not to giggle. "How may I help you?"

"Menus," we said, extending our hands daintily, wrists limp.

"Right away, madams!" she bellowed happily and galloped back inside.

She returned shortly, waving three menus. "Here they are!" she said proudly, smacking them down on the table. "Menus!"

Well, Joy might have put a pretty good effort into the decorations. But the menu left *a lot* to be desired!

"Peanut butter sandwich, grilled cheese sandwich, fried egg sandwich . . . Is that it?" I asked.

"What about drinks?" said Susan haughtily.

"Drinks? Oh yeah, *drinks!*" Joy whacked her hand on her forehead, snatched the menus out of our hands and ran back into the house, muttering, "Drinks, right . . . okay . . . excuse me, fancy ladies."

A moment later she was back.

"Drinks, fancy ladies," she said, wiping the sweat off her face with the back of her arm.

Susan ordered first. "Humm . . . Peppermint tea, milk, orange juice, and sugar water . . . humm . . . I'll have a grilled cheese sandwich and peppermint tea, please." Susan handed her menu to Joy.

"Me too," said Katie, handing her menu to Joy, who was proudly rocking back and forth. Chest puffed up. "Yes indeed! Most certainly! Fine ladies!" Beaming, just beaming all over.

But, I don't know, I just all of a sudden got all grouchy. Everyone pretending it was a proper menu when it wasn't. A real menu should have lots of choices. Lots! Not just three little piddly sandwiches. When I'm restaurant owner I fill the page with choices. And cook them if I have to.

So as I sat there, I got madder and madder until everybody had ordered, and they were all looking at me expectantly awaiting my order.

"Yes, fine lady?" said Joy happily.

"French fries," I said.

"What?" she asked, craning her neck forward like maybe her ears needed cleaning out.

"French . . . fries." I said it real slow and loud like she was deaf. *"I . . . want . . . french . . . fries."*

"But I . . . um . . . I . . ." she said, looking like she had swallowed a golf ball. "I . . . um . . . I . . . uh . . . the menu! Uh . . . fine lady . . . ummm . . . ahem . . . the menu!"

"Am I a fine lady or am I not!" I demanded.

"Uh yes . . . yes, you are a fine lady."

"Is this a restaurant or is it not?"

"Uh yes, yes it's a very fine restaurant!"

"Well then I . . . want . . . french . . . fries!"

There was this long silence, with Joy just standing there swallowing and blinking. Then she cleared her throat and said, "Ahem . . . Okay, fine lady," disappearing part of her lip under her teeth. Eyes big and worried. "I will get the cook to make french fries."

"I want french fries too!" squealed Katie excitedly.

"Okay," said Joy. "Two orders of french fries and one grilled cheese sandwich." And she went back into the house, twisting the sleeve of her apron around and around her finger.

We sat there awkwardly. Susan and Katie looking at me. Me not looking at them.

"That was mean!" said Susan accusingly.

"So!" I said, face hot, stomach hurting. "So!" I stared at them down my nose until they looked away.

We sat at the table for a very long time. Our dress-up clothes drooped. Hot and clammy. Grit and dust wafted over from the drive. Mosquitoes whined. And still we sat. Appetite gone. Fine ladies gone. We sat and waited. We waited for my french fries.

Then all of a sudden the screen door burst open and Joy came staggering out enveloped in clouds of black smoke. Her apron askew, her hair looking like a chicken had been scratching in it. Crumpled and dirty.

"I'm sorry, fine ladies," she said, tears rolling down her face. "I'm sorry for the delay . . . It's just . . ." Big gulping sobs. "It's just . . . the stove is on fire."

Then we all start screaming at once. We run inside, and sure enough flames are jumping all over the stove. So Susan grabs the box of baking soda and we throw handfuls of it at the stove. Finally the fire goes out and we stand there in our finery, coughing a little, bleary-eyed in the smoke. A thin film of baking soda covering everything, and Joy wringing her apron and crying.

"What a mess," says Katie. And Joy starts crying even louder. "Oh oh oh Daddy's gonna kill me! Ohhhh . . ."

Susan goes over and puts her arms around her.

"Don't worry," she says, "we'll clean it up and he will never know . . . Don't worry." Then she glares at me, and I start cleaning. I clean hard. And we cleaned it all up, and the grown-ups never knew.

Ice Cream for Breakfast

Mama was pregnant. Her tummy was getting bigger and fatter, and she drank a large glass of milk at every meal. She slept a lot too. Crawled into bed right after she got home from school.

And Daddy and her were always talking about how exciting it was. How we were going to have a baby brother or sister. But, I don't know. It wasn't that exciting. I've already got lots of brothers and sisters. Lots. And if they thought we needed another one, why didn't they just send for Faith? At least we're used to her. But I guess they didn't think of that, and so now Mama was pregnant, and her tummy was too big for hugs on her lap.

Then one night. A school night. We were upstairs. We were supposed to be asleep, but we were fooling around instead. So, as usual, Daddy called upstairs in his loud deep voice, "Who's awake up there?" Now what that means is "Who wants a spanking?" So of course we're all too smart to answer. We just leapt into bed and pulled the covers over our heads, hoping he'd go away. But he didn't. He just yelled even louder, *"Who's awake up there?"* So Katie squeaked, "I am, Daddy." Why? I don't know. But for some reason Katie always seems to answer, and then he makes her go downstairs and she gets a spanking. This happens every time. And every time I am flabbergasted! You'd think she would learn. But no!

"I am, Daddy."

"Then come down here at once!" he roared.

And so little Katie trotted downstairs all wide-eyed and pale.

Our ears all listened for the spanking, but it never came. Instead we heard the sound of the car starting up and driving away.

In the morning Mama was gone and Daddy was in the kitchen. He asked us what we wanted for breakfast and we said, "Ice cream!" So that's what we had. Ice cream for breakfast. Neapolitan. Then Daddy said, "Katie, I think you have something to tell your brothers and sisters."

"Yep," said Katie, eating her ice cream.

"What?" we asked impatiently.

But she just shook her head and made a big deal about how she couldn't talk with her mouth full. Not that it ever bothered her before.

"What, Katie?" Nick demanded.

"Weeeeellll," she said slowly, daintily dabbing her lips with her finger. "Weeellll . . ." Then it all came pouring out, in about five seconds flat.

"Mama had a baby, a baby brother, and I got to see it, I got to last night at the hospital, and I got to help choose its name and its name is William!"

Well I don't know about anyone else, but all of a sudden my ice cream lost its flavor.

"*What!* You got to see it *and* you got to *name it?*"

"Yep!" Katie said smugly.

"But that's not *fair!*"

"Yes it is!" sang Katie gleefully. "Daddy asked who was awake and I was the only one who answered! Just me! So I got to go."

"Yeah, but that's because I thought . . ." Then I noticed Daddy looking at me and decided I'd better shut up.

Three days later Mama came home with Baby Will. He was all wrinkly and red. Tiny too. With a patch of fuzzy black hair.

Wasn't much fun. Just cried and drank milk from Mama's breast. And slept. Slept a lot.

Mama thought we'd all like to taste her breast milk, so she squeezed some into a cup. I didn't really want to, but I didn't want to hurt her feelings, so I did. Didn't like it though.

Deep Freeze

I don't know what we would have done if someone hadn't invented the deep freeze. The deep freeze is a handy thing. And ours was even handier. You know how most people just have a little freezer on top of their fridge, and then sometimes if someone's lucky they have a deep freeze. Normal-sized usually. The size of a washing machine . . . Well we had a deep freeze. Not just a normal one either, but a big one. One the size of two washing machines stuck together, maybe even two and a half.

This deep freeze was mighty useful.

When there was a good deal on day-old bread, we'd

buy a whole bunch of it, maybe twelve loaves, and then freeze it! See, bread doesn't get older when it's frozen. It just stays the same age.

We'd also skim the cream off the top of the milk, mix it up with sugar and vanilla, wild strawberries if we could find them, and then stick it in the deep freeze. Every hour or so, we'd go down and stir it real good, until it was frozen. And boy let me tell you, it tasted great.

Nick used the deep freeze too. See, if we wanted meat, we had to kill it. Squirrels, rabbits, birds. Deer were the best. I always got bull's-eye on target practice. But somehow I always missed the animals. Once a deer came right up to me and nuzzled me. She had big brown eyes, warm breath. I brought my rifle up and pointed it at her as she turned and walked away. I followed her, keeping my bead trained on her until she disappeared into the woods on the other side of the meadow. I quickly fired a shot, but I must have missed her. Kind of disappointing too. Mama's birthday was coming up. I could have used the two dollars for a present. Nick usually missed targets, but he never missed deers. If he went out hunting, he always brought back one or two. He'd hang them by their hind legs from the pipes in the basement. First he'd take the skin off. Then he'd cut them open down the belly, plunge his hands in all the way past his elbows, and take all the innards out. Arms coated with thick crimson blood, face and T-shirt splattered. The warm smell of blood, animal and mildew from the basement all mixed up. He'd save the heart. We'd eat that. And he'd save the liver. Nobody ever ate when we had liver. It had too strong a flavor and a weird texture. We tried cooking it all sorts of ways. Fried in margarine and onions. Fried in catsup. Those were usually tried and true ways of making anything taste good. But the grown-ups were the only ones who could eat it. They'd smack their lips and say how tasty it was, how good for you, and how in many parts of the world, deer's liver was considered a delicacy. Delicacy or not, I couldn't eat it. The rest he'd chop up into sections. Ribs, legs, back. The scraps we'd grind up in the meat grinder. That was hard work. You'd have to attach the grinder to the table and then chop up all the scraps into little chunks, feed the chunks into one end, pump a handle around and around and around, and slowly, slowly, it would ooze out the other end. Then we'd wrap hamburger, back, ribs, and so on in brown paper and throw it in the deep freeze.

Now two deers sure wouldn't fit in a fridge, or a normal-sized deep freeze. That's why we were lucky to have a big one.

But the best thing about the deep freeze, or at least the thing I liked best about it, was its cooling factor.

There was nothing better on a hot summer day, than to play deep freeze. What you'd do is, you'd need another person. Because the lid's too heavy for one. So I usually got Joy or Katie to play with me. One of us would climb into the deep freeze, and lie down. The other would shut it, sit on the lid and count real slow. You'd try to see how long you could stay in there. And let me tell you this was no small feat, cause it was cold in there! And dark too! Then when you couldn't stand it anymore, you'd knock on the lid. They'd jump off, pull with their arms, you'd push from the inside with your feet, and it would open. Then you'd climb out, shivering, not just from cold, but also from the adventure.

Once Daddy called Joy when I was inside, and she

went upstairs and forgot all about me. It took me a long time to get out.

Abe

Abe's back. One day he's gone, never to be heard from again, and the next day, *boomp!* There he is, standing on our doorstep jaunty like. "Hi, Anna," he says. Like no time at all has passed. "Hi, Anna," he says eyes twinkling. "Is your mom in?"

He's much better-looking than he used to be. Not so pasty white and clammy. He has a beard. Reddish color. And his hair is longer and he has a tan.

I put my eyeballs back in my head and go get Mama.

She is just as speechless as I am. Just says, "Abe . . . Abe . . ." over and over again. And then she hugs him like she'll never stop. And I call all the kids, and we dance around and make a big deal.

Then Abe drives me and Katie and Susan into town in his new pickup truck. Actually, it's an old pickup truck. Chocolate color, rattly and rusty. But it's new to us, so it's pretty special. The seat is way high up in the air and you feel like you're on a throne or something.

"How'd you find us?" asks Katie.

"Magic . . ." he says, and winks at me, and I feel grown up.

Mama gave us some money to get the fixings for a hot dog roast to celebrate Abe's return.

When we got home, we built a big bonfire. We roasted hot dogs and marshmallows and Abe told us about his travels.

He was working the oil rigs up in *Alaska!* Alaska! Imagine that! I was pretty impressed. He kept on looking at Mama to see how she liked his stories, but she didn't seem to much, they just seemed to make her sort of sad.

Daddy was over at his friend Stan Fletcher's house. They like to play Ping-Pong. Stan Fletcher used to be some kind of champion player, but Daddy can keep up. Beats him once in a while. Funny how he still can't work, but he can play Ping-Pong.

Anyway, when Daddy came home from Stan's house, he looked pretty surprised to see Abe. Didn't hug him though. Just shook his hand and went inside. Didn't have a hot dog or anything.

Egg Surprise

Abe got a job at the pulp mill.

I wish Daddy would get a job there. Then maybe people would stop saying he's a layabout, and we'd have more money and I could have new clothes like all the other kids. But he won't. Says all those chemicals are bad for the lungs. Which is pretty hilarious coming from him, seeing as how he smokes constantly.

Anyway, you'd think Daddy would be happy about Abe's job, seeing as how Abe's pitching in for the family's expenses. But he's not. Every night when the grown-ups go to bed, Mama and Daddy start arguing.

"I want him out!"

"No."

"What do you mean no? I'm the man of the house and I want him out! I want him out now!"

"Stop yelling, you'll wake up the children."

"Fuck the children! It's the children I'm thinking of! You carrying on with them under the same roof. You think they don't notice? You think they're stupid?" There is a pause and then Mama speaks again. "We're not carrying on."

"Jean, I am not fucking stupid, you know what I mean? I'm not fucking stupid!" Then Mama cuts him off cold as ice. "Richard, he is staying. We need the money and I cannot raise the kids on what I make alone."

"I'll get a job. I'll support the family," says Daddy. And Mama starts laughing. Laughing kind of bitter like. "Yeah . . . right. You'll get a job! That's funny . . . that's very funny." And then Daddy starts crying and I hear Mama leave the bedroom and go outside.

Every night it's the same thing, over and over. "I want him out!" "No." "I'll get a job." "Ha . . . ha . . . ha . . ."

So anyway, Abe stays and Mama's happy and I make a box lunch for him when I make our school lunches. Only I make his fancier, cause he's a man and a grown-up.

I give him two sandwiches. Peanut butter and jelly. And he doesn't mind. Says he likes them, which is a good thing, cause that's mainly what we have.

And I pick a real good apple from the king apple tree, cause they're really big and crunchy and sweet. I make sure to pick him the very best one and check it all over for worm holes.

He also really likes boiled eggs. So I boil them up the night before and let them cool in the fridge.

Then I top it all off with piping hot instant coffee. Taster's Choice.

The thermos he has can keep coffee hot up to twelve hours! And it looks like it too. All silver metal, with little ridges, probably for the heat, and breakable glass inside.

I pack it all up in his black metal lunch box, and it looks so professional. And when he goes to work everyone is jealous of his fancy lunches. And he holds up my boiled eggs and says, "Ahhh! Nice brown farm eggs, laid fresh this morning!" And then he cracks the egg on his forehead with mighty gusto, peels it, sprinkles a little salt on it and gobbles it up!

Well . . . one morning I must have gotten the boiled

eggs and the raw eggs mixed up. And so when he smacked what he thought was a hard-boiled egg on his forehead with mighty gusto it went *splat!* And he went gurgle, splutter, as the raw egg went running down his face.

And he didn't even get mad at me. Just laughed and laughed and laughed and laughed. Long and loud.

Kept laughing about it for days after. Shaking his head and wiping tears from his eyes. "And there I was," he said, "trying to look dignified, with raw egg pouring down my face."

Gone Again

Abe's gone. Daddy beat him up so he left.

Here's what happened.

I woke up. It was the middle of the night. Dark. Pitch black. Only a skinny fingernail of a moon. And I'm lying there, eyes wide, heart pounding. Scared and I don't know why. Lying there, staring into the darkness. So dark I can barely see the white cottage cheese ceiling of my room. White with blackish red smears from squashed mosquitoes.

And yet, somehow I can see Abe. See him in my head. Walking down the road. Whistling softly, swinging his black metal lunch box. And I am scared.

"Go back . . . go back," I whisper. But of course he

can't hear me, cause he's too far away. Half a mile maybe. Walking . . . closer . . . closer . . . Down the hill now . . . Over the bridge.

"Go back! Go back!" I am screaming. And yet my room is quiet. So quiet. And I am just lying there. Still, body shivering, not making a noise.

Up the hill he comes, along the drive. I can hear him whistling for real now. And I am crying, cause I know it's too late.

Then there is a roar, Daddy bursts outside, and I lose the picture of Abe. And all I hear is Daddy yelling. "You motherfucker! You son of a bitch! And this is how you pay back my hospitality! You son of a bitch!" And I hear hitting noises and kicking noises, and "Ooph" noises, and Mama crying.

"You're fucking my wife!" Daddy yells. And I put the pillow over my head and sing "Happy Birthday" so I can't hear anymore.

Menstruation

They were learning about menstruating and periods and things in Life class. I wasn't allowed to go. Mama refused to sign my permission slip. She said my teacher was evil, evil, evil, and she was not going to have me taught things and discussing things like that. Mama said those things were family business, and that she'd teach us what we'd need to know.

So every other day after lunch I had to go outside and play on the playground with the boys while the girls stayed inside with the teacher. I was the only girl outside. I hated it!

This was one time the boys didn't make fun of me, they seemed to be shy or something. During the time outside, they didn't play with me or speak to me. They just kind of looked through me. Like I didn't exist. I was one of "them." But I wasn't.

When the teacher unlocked the door, the boys and I'd creep back in. The girls, a noisy quiet. Flushed, secretive, a club. A club I didn't belong to. I pretended I didn't care. I pretended disdain. That I already knew about menstruations and periods and things like that . . . But I didn't.

My sisters, shy about asking Mama to tell us, didn't say anything. Not me. I asked her. She tried to avoid the subject, but I kept asking her. I asked again and again and again.

One morning when Daddy was in town getting groceries and Nick and Matthew were outside, Mama called us girls into her bedroom. We all filed in. Mama was flushed . . . fluttery . . . mysterious. She shut the bedroom door and told us to sit down. Then she went to her underwear drawer and got out a white elastic band. It had two dangly bits on it. She stood there for a moment, holding it, as if she somehow forgot why she was there standing in front of us.

"What's that, Mama?" asked Katie. I didn't know either, but pretended I did.

Mama stopped looking at the thing and swung her head vaguely over in our direction. Her eyes skittering over our heads, resting finally on the apple tree out her window. She cleared her throat and then said, "It's a belt . . . a belt . . . It's a belt you use when you are menstruating. It is to hold the pads on." Then she dropped it back into her underwear drawer and shut it. She went to her closet and brought out a big pale blue box with a printed white lace pattern on it. It said "Maxi Pads. Super absorbent. 48 pads." "And these are the pads," she said. "You use these with the belt. I keep the belts in here and the pads in there. If any of you start menstruating, this is where you'll find them." Mama looked relieved now that she was talking. "Now," she continued, "you may also have heard of something called a tampon. I would not recommend these. They are very painful and often get stuck up there. My friend Marilyn tried to use them after her wedding night. She couldn't find the string and her husband had to be called home from the office to get it out!" Mama giggled. "It was very embarrassing to say the least . . ." She laughed again with her social face, wafting her arm outward from her body. We laughed too. Red . . . embarrassed. Pretending to understand.

Then Mama paused and looked at us. Looked at us real hard through her glasses. "There is one more thing we need to discuss." The words came out slow . . . so slow and deliberate. "Good girls don't . . . and bad girls do . . . Do I make myself clear?" I nodded with my sisters. Scared by the tone of her voice, the almost angry ferocity, embarrassment of the conversation, the closeness of the air.

She stared at us for a minute longer and then her face cleared.

"All right that's all, you can go." She opened the bedroom door and we scampered out. Out of the bedroom to freedom, fresh air, sunshine.

Our eyes slip away from one another. My curiosity replaced with a kind of dirty feeling inside, guilty. None of us discuss it.

I was washing the breakfast dishes when I heard kind of a scream. My body got that racing tummy knot stillness. I don't know how I knew, but I knew. I ran into the bathroom. My hands still hot and soapy wet from the dishwater. Susan was sitting on the toilet, crying, crying. I pulled her close, hugging her. Stroking her hair. "It's okay, Susan . . . It's okay."

I stayed with her until her sobs became hiccups. Then I sneaked into Mama's bedroom and stole an elastic belt and some pads.

We didn't tell anybody. We didn't talk about it. I took the dirty undies outside and hid them deep in the garbage cans. Far down in the garbage so no one would know, my love for Susan bursting.

The Burglar

Katie stayed home from school. The thing about staying home from school, was not to let Daddy know you were staying home. Cause then he would make you do lots of work and act funny with you.

So sometimes Katie hid under the sofa in the living room, until Daddy had checked out the bedrooms to see who was home. And then when he went out, she would creep upstairs. Or she would hide on the top shelf of the closet, which was her bedroom. She would surround herself with her stuffed toys. And when Daddy would come upstairs to check if anyone was home, she would hold her breath and not move a muscle until he was gone.

Well today she hid in the top shelf of the closet.

She could hear his footsteps. "Clump . . . clump . . ." as he came up the stairs. She could hear his breathing. She heard Susan and Joy's bedroom door open. She could hear him moving around, opening cupboards. Then she heard him move down the hall. "Clump . . . clump . . ." It was quiet, so he must just be looking in the doorway. "Clump . . . clump . . ." Now he was coming towards her closet! Check, yes, stuffed animals in place! Katie's heart was pounding. Her mouth dry. She was scared . . . But it was an exciting scared . . . "Clump . . . clump . . ." Now it was time to hold her breath. She held it and squeezed her eyes shut. She knew shutting her eyes wouldn't help. But somehow, there was that belief that if she couldn't see him . . . then he couldn't see her. She knew he was in the doorway now. She didn't move . . . she didn't breathe . . . She could hear him come in the closet, moving around, checking the lumps in the bedding. Her lungs were exploding. Finally he left.

She could breathe . . . She didn't move yet . . . he might hear her. But what a surge of joy! She won! She won! He didn't know she was home! Chalk one up for clever Katie! What a victory!

She lay there crouched on the top shelf for a long time, waiting for Daddy to go out. He usually went out. But today he didn't. He went into his bedroom, which was at the foot of the stairs. When was he going to come out? He didn't come out, and he didn't come out, and he didn't come out! Katie was getting hungry.

All of a sudden she heard a squeaking, creaking noise. That was strange. Then she heard a low moaning sound. What was it? Was it Daddy?

"Mooooan . . ." Squeak . . . creak . . .

"Mooooooooaaan . . ." Louder this time. What was it? Katie was getting worried. Was Daddy okay? Was he hurt? Were there burglars torturing him? Was he *dying?*

"Ahhhhmooooaaann!"

That was it. She was going down to help him! She grabbed her water pistol full of pee, that she kept expressly in case a burglar incident should arise. She went down the stairs as quietly as she could. The thing about burglars is, you have to catch them by surprise.

"Mooooaan . . . Aaahhhh!" Squeak . . . squeak . . . She was by his bedroom door now. She could feel her face flush. Her heart beating. She took a big breath and flung

135

open the door! Water pistol of pee ready. But there was no burglar . . . nobody but Daddy. And he was lying on his back with his legs in the air, holding on to his penis! But the funniest thing of all is that he was wearing maroon nylons, bits of his hair from his legs were poking through . . . *and* not only that . . . *He was wearing Mama's pink see-through negligee!*

And if that wasn't strange enough . . . something even stranger happened. It was quite a warm day . . . but suddenly Daddy got cold. Real cold. Cause he jumped off the bed yelling *"Aahhhhh!"* And grabbed the quilt and wrapped it around him. Tight. Yep, he must have been cold. So cold that his face turned red.

Well he made Katie promise, promise, promise that she wouldn't tell anybody! Anybody at all!

And he must have really meant it too. Cause he gave her *fifty cents!* And Daddy never gives money to anybody.

So Katie took the fifty cents, and promised she wouldn't tell *anybody*. And you know how I know? Cause she told me! Right when I got home from school.

And we laughed and laughed about it. Grown-ups sure are weird. Anyway Katie and I walked down to Mary's cafe, and she gave me half of her money and we each got twenty-five Bozos. They sure were good.

Smoking Salems

Daddy smokes Salems. Salem menthols. Five packs a day. Drinks red wine too. Great big jugs of it. Sometimes when company's over, he gives us kids a swig. Tastes bitter, but I take a real big gulp. Swallow it whole, act as if I like it so people'll think I'm grown up.

He doesn't offer us cigarettes. Doesn't need to though, cause I already know how to smoke.

At first I learned on candy cigarettes. I would save up my money and then on real cold days I'd buy some and sit across from the school where the big kids sat and smoked their real cigarettes.

The fence was pretty high and teetery. But I'm a good climber. So I'd clamber up and perch on the top rung, feet hooked under the second. Precariously balanced, smoking my candy cigarettes, nibbling them down so they got smaller, like real cigarettes. My breath puffing out warm clouds of steam.

I looked real cool. On my smoking days I always made sure I was wearing my jeans and jean jacket. Once I wore a dress, but one of the big kids pushed me, and I fell and they could see my underwear. They all laughed and laughed, figuring I'd never come back. But it just made me more determined. After that I would only buy candy cigarettes. No Bozos, no shoelaces, no strawberries, just candy cigarettes.

So they gave up and pretty much left me on my own.

Once Robbie Pletzer shook the fence real hard and made it sway and wobble, but I just held on tight and yelled at the top of my lungs, *"Ride em, cowboy! Wheeee!"* Like it was a real fun ride. He got embarrassed and stopped. Kicked the fence and went to smoke somewhere else. I was glad, cause I was scared.

Gradually they all went. Every day a few more gone, until finally, I was the only one left.

It was kind of lonely sitting on that big fence all by myself smoking my candy cigarettes.

I felt kind of foolish, so I stopped.

Susan was glad. She didn't like me doing it. Acted like I was trying to ruin her life or something. Said I was stupid, a fool, and a humiliation to the family. Maybe I was, but I couldn't help it.

Then one day when Daddy was out, Katie, Joy and I decided we were going to smoke. Really smoke.

We stole Daddy's abalone ashtray. Snuck it up to our tree house.

Our tree house was near the top of a big pine tree. The biggest pine tree on all the property. It was real high up and behind the barn. So you could do the sneakiest things and the grown-ups would never know. First of all they never had any reason to go in the barn, let alone behind it. And secondly, neither one of them was a tree climber, and the ladder only went halfway up the tree.

So that's why we brought Daddy's ashtray to the tree fort. It was full of cigarette butts, maybe thirty or forty of them when we left the house. But by the time we got to the fort, there were only twelve.

I divided them, so I got last choice, which wasn't quite fair, cause there were only two long ones.

In our excitement we'd forgotten matches, so we sent Katie back for them. She was pretty brave about it. Ran real fast. Actually, considering she had bare feet, she practically flew. Dodging boulders, prickles, leaping over stumps.

When she came back she was puffing hard. Matches in her teeth, scrambled up, scraped her knee, a few drops of blood forming. But she didn't even seem to care. Which was real unusual. Normally the tiniest little scratch and she's rolling on the floor and screaming bloody murder.

But not this time. "Matches!" she said proudly and smacked them on the floor. "Matches!" Then she flopped on her back, breathing hard.

The wind was really creaking the trees.

"Okay," I said. "Who wants to go first?"

"You can," said Katie, panting. "I'm too out of breath!"

I looked at Joy. I kind of hoped she would, but she just looked at me and nibbled her thumbnail with the side of her mouth.

So I said in a voice that was too loud for my ears, "Oh good! That means I get to go first!" I made a big show out of choosing my cigarette butt, straightened it out. Put it in my mouth. Not the whole thing. Just the very end of it. What you do is you make a hole with your lips like you're trying to whistle, then you put the cigarette in and tighten your lips around it so it won't fall out. I know, cause I've practiced alot.

"Matches, where are the matches?" I said. They were

right in front of me, but if I had to go first, I was going to make the most of it.

Katie handed them to me. Eyes big. She wasn't out of breath anymore.

I lit the match and put the flame on the end of the cigarette butt. I held it there for a long time. It was hot, but the butt didn't catch fire.

"You have to suck on it!" said Katie. "You have to suck on it to make it catch. That's what Daddy does!"

"Yeah!" said Joy.

"I know!" I said. "I was only practicing!" Then I lit another match and sucked . . . and . . . *I smoked!* I really did! Katie and Joy cheered and I coughed and took it out of my mouth.

"It's good," I said, still coughing. "It tastes like mint-flavored! Yum! It's good!" And then I took another puff to show them. It was a combination of raggity rough and cool mint in the throat.

They lit theirs and we all puffed and coughed with watery eyes.

All that smoke made me feel a little dizzy.

When we had smoked all our cigarette butts, we wobbled down the ladder and staggered home.

Daddy wasn't home yet, so we quickly washed out his ashtray and stuck it back on the living room table and went upstairs to bed.

Matthew

This has not been what I'd call a great week for Matthew. First off he got in three fights this week. Actually, only one qualifies as a fight. The other two there was fighting involved; he just got beaten up. He gets beaten up all the time, I don't know why. Maybe it's on account of his red hair or something. And then to top it all off, he starts getting his real bad asthma attacks. I daydream about sneaking into Mama's purse and stealing some medicine for him. But I don't. If it was Daddy's medicine I would for sure. It's strange really, though Matthew is in grade seven, three grades above me, I always feel like I've got to take care of him. Protect him. He's not aware that I do this, but I do.

Like when we would play plops. A game that's sort of like kick the can, except when you step in cow poop you have to scream "Plops!" And it makes it easier for whoever is It to find you. And the only other difference is you have a partner. Well, everybody always wanted to be Nick or Susan's partner. They'd clamor around them saying, "Please . . . Please, me!" "No, me!" "No, you got to go with them last time!"

Now, Matthew's the same age as Nick, but nobody wanted to be Matthew's partner. Nobody.

So I'd crowd around him and say, "Me, Matthew! Me . . . Can I be your partner? Please?" I'd say all this loud and move around alot. Loud so he wouldn't realize I was the only one asking, and moving alot so as to give the impression there was more than one person.

Then he'd say, "No, Anna, you were my partner last time . . . you have to give someone else a chance." He'd look around for someone else.

But everyone else was still clamoring around Susan and Nick. They were fun, they were exciting, they were inventive, risk takers, daring. Matthew tried to be, but he just wasn't.

Then he'd say loud, "Who wants to be my partner?" Nobody would answer. So I would say even louder, "Me! Me! Matthew! I want to be your partner! *Please!*" And so he'd sigh and say, "All right. Come on, Anna . . . God what a pest." And off he'd stomp, me scampering behind him.

Matthew and I were still running. We were, by this time, way out in the second meadow. He always liked to hide far away. That way he could be daring, rattle branches, do coyote howls, without risking getting caught by whoever was It.

But what Matthew didn't understand was, that risking things was what made it fun.

My right side of my stomach felt like it was going to split right open and my guts were going to burst all over the second meadow. This had me a little nervous, but I didn't want to ruin Matthew's fun. So I didn't say anything. I just grabbed my side and held it tight together, punching my fists inwards slightly against my ribs. Hopefully that would hold my guts in.

We ran on. The tall dry grass slashing against my bare thighs, itching my legs.

"Okay," Matthew whispered hoarsely. "This is far enough." And he dove headfirst into the tall grass. I stopped gratefully. I don't know why he was whispering. We were miles away from anyone.

I felt a whack on my leg. I looked down. Matthew was lying on his stomach.

"Hit the ground!" he hissed urgently through his teeth. He always said that, "Hit the ground." I don't know why, but I always had the impulse to bend over and punch the ground with my fist. I didn't though. I didn't think Matthew would find it very amusing.

I flopped onto my stomach. I could smell the damp dark earth. It was cool. The grass was scratchy. I could hear Matthew wheezing beside me. He made kind of whistling noises as the air rattled through his lungs.

I always felt awkward when Matthew had his asthma. I never knew quite what I should do. I knew he thought it was a weakness. Something he should be able to stamp out if he was strong like Nick.

But he couldn't stamp it out, he always had asthma, just like Mama. Only Mama was allowed to have medicine and he wasn't.

I never look at him when he has it. Cause he would see that I feel sorry for him, that I'm worried. And if he ever saw that, I know he would never forgive me.

So I just pretended I couldn't hear him wheezing. I rolled over on my back and looked at the sky. It was almost a full moon.

I started talking about how clever he was to find this hiding place. How nobody would ever find us. How much fun it was to be his partner . . . Careful not to ask any questions, so he wouldn't have to answer. I listened closely. Yes, Matthew's wheezing was getting softer. Thank you, God. I didn't really believe in God. But I tried always to think good thoughts and thank Him regularly, just in case there was one. I talked some more, softly. Then finally I stopped. Matthew's asthma had subsided a bit.

I still didn't look at him. Finally he rolled onto his stomach and crawled over to a blackberry bramble bush.

I waited. Did he need to throw up? Did he need to pee? I pretended to look at the stars.

"Anna . . . come on . . . hurry up," he said impatiently.

Oh . . . We were playing the game.

Relieved, I scrambled over. When I got there Matthew howled. *"Ararawhooo . . ."* I guess now it was coyote howling time.

"Ararawooooooo," I howled. We ran to another bush and howled again.

Then we scrambled up a tree and started to rattle the branches and hoot like barn owls.

We sounded pretty good and scary. I sat up there in the tree and listened to the far-off faint sounds of shrieks and laughter. It would be so much fun, if only we had an audience to scare.

We ran from bush to bush and tree to tree. Howling and hooting. Hooting and howling. We never got close to anyone. And no one ever got close to us. Finally it was time to go in.

As I lay in bed I listened to my sisters recounting the glorious events of the night. The close calls, the narrow escapes, the scares. When Nick leapt out from behind a bush and roared right in Susan and Joy's faces. And they were so scared they grabbed each other instead of him. And he got away.

"Where were you hiding anyway?" Susan demanded.

"In the hayloft, under the hay! You guys walked right over us and never noticed!" said Katie, hugging herself with glee.

"And how about when I stepped in the cow pooh!" said Joy happily, "and it went right over my zorries!"

"In between your toes! And we had to go down to the creek and wash it off!"

"*Eeeyeeww!*"

They talked on and on.

I thought about Matthew, how he had his asthma. How excited he was after the game was over and we were running home. Waving his skinny arms about, his hair all tousled. Saying gleefully over and over again, "Nobody even got close! Nobody even got close! They had no idea! No idea! None!" Wheezing a little from the exertion and excitement. His face blotchy.

My sisters were quieter now . . . An occasional whisper . . . a giggle . . . And I lay there thinking.

Lord of the Rings

Matthew's not supposed to read fairy tales. I don't know why he does. He always gets in bad trouble when Daddy finds out. But he still does it.

I was in the kitchen doing the dishes. Mountains of dishes. Nine people in the house, there's bound to be a lot of dishes. Then Daddy started yelling. My tummy seized up into little hard knots. When Daddy started yelling like that it meant somebody was going to get it.

I started clanging the dishes louder and humming "Happy Birthday" so I wouldn't hear him so good. I could still hear him, but at least this way I couldn't make out what he was yelling, or if he was yelling for me. Now I could hear the sound of someone being hit, hurting noises.

I rattled and hummed a bit louder.

Katie scurried into the kitchen carrying a stack of dishes. Her hair hadn't been brushed forever and had become one big rat's nest at the back. She gets rat's nests all the time. That's because her hair's so fine.

Her eyes and mouth made little round worried O's. "Daddy's beating up Matthew," she whispered. My heart skipped.

"Why?"

"Because he was reading those fairy tales again . . .

Lord of the Rings . . . Daddy found it under his mattress. He's really hurting him!"

I was scared. I ran into the living room. Heart pounding. Daddy was holding Matthew with one arm and beating him with a piece of kindling with the other. Without thinking I grabbed his arm and started yelling and crying at the same time. "Daddy, stop! Please stop! Stop, Daddy!" Daddy tried to get rid of me, but I wouldn't let go.

Suddenly Matthew turned on me with betrayed trapped eyes, and yelled through clenched teeth, "Get lost, Anna! Just get lost!" I froze. I turned around and slowly started back to the kitchen.

"Anna . . . Anna, wait," I heard Daddy call, his voice challenging me in a way, taunting me. I stopped. "Come here, I want to show you something." There were rushing noises in my ears, my whole body was an enormous weight. I couldn't move. "No," I whispered.

"What did you say?"

I didn't answer.

"Anna!"

Slowly I turned around. "What?"

"I said come here. I want to show you something."

Slowly I walked back. Hot and cold. Now I was standing in front of him.

"What."

"Matthew, take off your pants." Matthew slowly did, looking down. I lowered my eyes. I would not watch. Daddy hit me across the face. "Look!" he demanded. I looked. Matthew's penis was all purple and small. His body was skinny. You could see all his ribs. I had never seen Matthew naked before. He had red blotches and scabs from other beatings. And he was all bluish red. He was shivering, but I don't think it was from the cold.

His eyes cast down. Arms hanging limply, ending in little tight fists.

I started to cry. I couldn't help it.

Then Daddy started to laugh. He laughed and laughed and laughed.

"Anna," he said, "I just wanted to show you my new way of breaking kindling!"

Then he picked up a piece of kindling and beat Matthew with it until it broke.

"Thank you, Matthew," he would say, and then he would pick up another piece and start all over again.

Matthew standing there. Red welts rising. Blood dripping. Fists, eyes, jaw clenched. Determined not to cry out, and Daddy determined that he will.

The next morning I got up real early. I don't know how I knew, but I did. I went outside to the green truck. The back of the truck was open, the doors slapping gently from the movement inside. I ducked down low, crouching almost, and made my way over to the cherry tree, better view. I hid behind it and watched. Watched Mama stuffing all of Matthew's things in a big black garbage bag. Nick pretending to be asleep, Matthew standing there all stiff-backed. Just standing there looking kind of lost, watching Mama.

Then Mama came out.

"Come on, Matthew," she called. "Let's get a move on." But Matthew just stood there.

"Come on, Matthew. You've got a long drive ahead of you."

"Where's he going?" I yelled from behind the tree.

Mama looked caught for a minute, and then she started chirping gaily about how Matthew was going to go on a "little trip" to see his dad and Jeremy! Lucky Matthew! But she didn't fool me. I knew they were sending him away. Sending him away forever. Just like Faith.

I kissed Matthew good-bye, and tried to act like before, like he was my big exciting hero. Making a big noisy fuss. But he didn't look at me, and I didn't look at him. Because we both knew I was faking.

I made my mouth smile, and yelled, "Good-bye, Matthew!" Good and loud as Daddy and Matthew drove away. Waving real big. But he didn't turn around. And the van got smaller and smaller and then it disappeared.

Mama wanted to hug me. But I made my shoulders all stiff so she let go. Then I went upstairs, crawled into bed with all my clothes on and pulled the covers over my head. Over my head and around my body. Tight, tight, tight, to try and stop the shaking.

Four

Cecilia

It was mine and Katie's week for laundry and the whole basement stank.

I'd put in a load of reds on Monday and here it was Thursday before we remembered. And boy did it stink. Stank of mildew.

"It's your fault!" said Katie.

"Is not!" I said. "I put them in so it was your job to hang them out!"

"Was not," said Katie.

"Was too," I replied.

"Was not."

"Was too."

It was a real boring argument. Neither one of us very

passionate. But also neither one willing to back down in case Mama smelled the mildew and got us in trouble.

"Was not."

"Was too . . ."

"Was not . . ."

"Was too . . ." I flopped on my back on the mound of whites. Katie flopped on the huge stack of darks.

"Was not . . ." she said. I knew how stubborn she was, and I knew how stubborn I was, so I just lay there on the dirty laundry and stared up at the tangle of sewer pipes swarming all over the ceiling.

Somebody flushed the toilet. Probably Daddy. He poohs a lot. And we could hear it gurgling and sucking through the pipes. I like to try to figure out which pipe the stuff is going through. I want to be a plumber when I grow up. They are real rich, and I'm good at that kind of stuff.

Whenever the toilet's broken I fix it. If it's clogged, I try the plunger. And if that doesn't work then I get out the snake and stick it way down in the toilet. Way down, and I wiggle it around. Around and around and up and down. Kind of like I'm beating a cake. Beating a cake and spearing a fish. Generally that does the trick, and the toilet is as good as new. And if the toilet won't flush and just makes a running water sound it could be two things. One, the floating ball thing that is attached to a metal thing is stuck in the up position. In that case you just take off the lid and push it down. Or two, the metal clasp that pulls the plunger plug on the bottom has either fallen off or is broken. If it has fallen off, you just put it back on. And if it has broken, you make another one. You can use a piece of wire or a hairpin, anything strong that can bend.

I've fixed the toilet many times. If I was a plumber, I'd be rich.

So anyway I lay on the dirty laundry and listened to the pooh go down the pipes.

Katie was listening too. Trying to track it, wasn't paying any attention to me, so I whispered, "Was not." Real quiet, so she couldn't hear, and that was the end of that. She thought she'd won, and I knew I had.

The victory gave me a surge of energy.

"Okay, let's get to it." I jumped up and started shoveling the stinky laundry into the laundry basket. "Hop to it, Katie. Start up the darks!"

"What are you doing with that?"

"Gonna hang it up to dry." It already was pretty dry, kind of stiff. Stiff little wrinkled lumps of clothes.

"But it stinks!" she said.

"So we air it out."

She didn't answer, just shook her head in amazement.

"What?" I said impatiently. "Do you want to do an extra load?"

"No . . ."

"Then hop to it."

She dragged herself off the stack of dirty clothes and started putting them in the washing machine and I went outside to hang up the clothes.

I shook the lumps, but they pretty much stayed in the shape they were in.

Katie didn't come out and help, but I didn't really expect her to.

I went back in. She was lying on the stack of whites this time. The washing machine chugging away.

"Anna?" she said. "Anna . . . has Nick ever tried to play grown-ups with you?"

I just looked at her. She wasn't supposed to know about things like that.

"Huh? Has he?"

"What do you mean?" I asked suspiciously.

"Grown-ups. You know, grown-ups! Where he tries to do things to you."

"What kind of things?"

"You know . . . kissing and stuff."

"You kissed Nick?"

"Not mmeee! I didn't *do* it! But has he ever tried with you?"

"Has he ever tried with you?" I asked. Cause I sure wasn't gonna tell her he tried with me if he hadn't tried with her, cause she'd throw it back at me later.

"I asked you first," she said, looking away. And I could tell he had. So I said, "Yeah, he tried with me once." She sat up and looked at me.

"When?"

"You tell me first cause I told you first."

She knew I had her. So she told me. She was acting embarrassed, but at the same time kind of proud. "Three and a half weeks ago, Nick and me were having a hay fight. We were rolling around and he was stuffing hay in my top, in my face, in my pants and everything, and then he pulled my pants down. Undies and all. He pretended it was an accident, but then he pulled his pants down, and I saw his penis! And he asked me if I wanted to play grown-ups."

"Did you?"

"No! Of course not! Yuck!"

I don't know what I was feeling. But it was a mixture

of something. Relief? Disappointment? Envy? I don't know.

The kitchen sink pipes were going now.

"He put his penis in my bellybutton once," I said.

"Eeewwww! What did it feel like?"

"Oh," I said casually, "it felt kind of like a finger. A round finger." I flopped down beside her on the laundry heap. Careful not to let our bodies touch. Don't know why, cause normally it wouldn't bother me.

We were quiet for a while. Then Katie said, "I wonder what it's like to play grown-ups . . . I wonder what they do?"

"I don't know," I said. I was wondering too.

"Nick knows," said Katie.

"Ummm . . ." I said.

"Maybe we should ask him," said Katie.

"Ummm . . ." I said.

We were quiet for a while longer. Then Katie said, "You ask him."

"Nah," I said. "You ask him."

"Nah," Katie said.

We were quiet again.

"Maybe if we sang him a song?" said Katie.

"What song?" I said.

"Umm . . . What about 'L is for the way you look at me'?"

"No." I thought for a moment. Then it hit me, inspiration! "What about 'Cecilia'!" The second I said it I knew there was no going back. That was it! "Go get him!"

"Why me?" said Katie.

"Because I thought of the song."

"What do I say?"

"Tell him we have something to say to him. And then

when he gets here, we'll sing it to him!" We avoided each other's eyes. I knew my face was flushed. Katie's too. She left and I waited.

When Katie came back she had Nick with her. "Well?" he said impatiently. "What do you want?" Katie and I looked at each other. She didn't say anything and neither did I. "What?" he demanded. He was grouchy. Not romantic at all. I didn't want to do it anymore. My tummy was hurting. But here was Nick, waiting for an answer, and I'd told Katie I was going to, so I started singing.

"Ceceeeeyilya I'm down on my knees I'm beggin' you please to come home . . ." I elbowed Katie and she started singing too. Shuffling her feet. Looking down at her toes.

"Makin' love in the afternoon with Ceceeeeyilya up in my-high bedroom. I go downstairs to waaaahhhash my face, when I come back to bed someone's takin' my place . . ." We trailed off, hearts loud, faces hot. We didn't look at Nick. It was quiet. So quiet. I felt real stupid.

"You mean it?" he said.

We nodded. Katie slipped her hand in mine.

"You sure?"

"Uh huh . . ." we said.

"Okay," he said efficiently. "Who's first?"

Neither one of us moved.

"Who's first?" he said again.

We didn't answer. So he said, "Okay, pull straws. Longest one goes first."

Katie got the longest.

"All right," said Nick, pointing at me. "You go up-stairs."

"Upstairs?" squeaked Katie, her hand tightening in mine.

"Yeah. Upstairs! What do you think? I'm gonna do it with an audience? Go on! Get outta here!"

I didn't know what to do, so I left.

I couldn't tell anybody. I was scared. Being alone wasn't part of the deal. Maybe I should've gone first. After all I was ten. One and a half years older than Katie. I could handle things better. What if Katie got hurt! What if Nick wanted to do something she didn't want him to! Helpless. Couldn't do anything . . . Couldn't protect Katie. Little jut-out-chin Katie . . . Then all of a sudden I remembered! The heating vents! You could hear through them! Hear people in the basement! I ran upstairs to my bedroom, opened the vent. Opened it wide. It was real dusty. I lay down on the floor and pressed my ear right up against it. I had to concentrate, but I could hear them. Real faint. Like they were in a tunnel, a million miles away. Couldn't hear everything. Just a mumbling, and a word every once in a while. Drifting up, drifting, floating like dandelion puffs. "Take . . ." "What . . ." "I don't . . ." "Because . . ." Words floating, drifting. Me listening, eavesdropping, feeling dirty.

Then "No." "Shush." "Don't . . ." Words louder now, clearer. "Don't, Nick! Don't, it'll hurt!" "Shush! Don't be such a baby!" Crying, I hear crying. Nick speaking. Angry voice. "Stop it! Stop crying!" Now Katie. "Nooo . . . It'll hurt!"

"Hush! You want to get me in trouble! *Hold still!*"

I ran. I ran downstairs as fast as I could. Slammed the basement door and stood there panting. Didn't know what

159

I was going to do. Knew I had to stop it. Nick jumped off of Katie and pulled his pants up.

"*Jesus Christ!*" he yelled. "I *told* you to wait *upstairs!*"

Katie was crying. He looked down at her and then yelled real loud. "*Are you guys ever stupid!*" And then he stomped outside and slammed the door. And when Katie stopped crying we finished the laundry.

Bath Day

Bathtime at our house was not an everyday occurrence. It was an event. Around once a month Mama would decide it was "bath day."

Baths were taken in order of age, and who was around. If you missed it you just had to wait until the next "bath day."

Daddy had first dibs. He usually didn't take one. But if he did decide to, we'd all try to make sure we weren't around, cause he'd call us in and make us clean him. It was pretty embarrassing. He'd always try to get us to clean all of him. But I'd always just say no. I'd just help him with his back. After all he could reach the rest by himself.

When he had finished Mama would disappear into the bathroom. She liked to stay in the tub for a long time.

Sometimes over an hour. Until the water turned gray and lukewarm around her, with little flecks of dead skin floating on the surface. Mama would emerge with her hair wrapped in a towel and another towel wrapped around her body. Her face would be flushed and groggyish looking, like when she'd had too much wine. Kind of unfocused eyes. Her body would have red scratch marks all over her, from where she was trying to scrape herself clean. She'd walk back to her bedroom in kind of mincing little steps, with her feet curled up so they wouldn't have to touch the floor much. Cause our floor is kind of dirty. Mama, balanced precariously on her skinny little chicken legs. Skinny little chicken legs with big knobby knees and purple spider tracks all over them. It's kind of strange how Mama got such a big tummy after having Baby Will and yet her legs stayed so skinny.

Nick refused to take a family bath. He thought it was disgusting. He washed at friends' houses or in the creek.

So then it would be Susan's turn.

I used to take a bath with Katie. But Daddy started bugging Susan in the bathtub, try to wash her bottom and soap her all up and stuff. It made her scared, so she asked if I'd take my baths with her.

Katie got real upset when she found out.

"And *who*," she roared, "am I going to play slippery-slide with!"

"Baby Will," I said.

"I don't want to take a bath with Baby Will. He pees in the tub!"

"Joy then."

"No!" she wailed. "Joy doesn't like to play slippery-slide! *It's not fair!*"

I felt bad, but there was nothing I could do, so I said, "Tough titties," and left.

So now I take a bath with Susan, cause Daddy can't try anything when there are two of us.

He just comes in and sits on the toilet. Usually pretending he has something interesting to read us. It's never interesting, and always long. Lots of times he'll just read a sentence or two and then sit and stare for a while before he reads some more. We're lucky we have long hair, cause we can cover our tops. But covering our bottoms is more difficult. It would be easier if we had washcloths like normal families. Once I had the smart idea to put towels in the tub! Pretending it was a game. But Daddy complained to Mama, and we got in trouble for misusing family property. It's too bad too, cause those towels covered us real well.

The water was pretty lukewarm when we got to it, so I hate to think what it was like when it finally got down to Baby Will's turn . . .

I liked staying overnight at my friend Lynn's house. We got to be the only ones to use the water. Good and hot too! She was lucky. She got to take a bath every night if she wanted to!

Therapy

Mama and Daddy have this new thing. They decided that us kids are screwed up and need to go into therapy. So Mama took the ferry to the mainland and got a whole slew of psychology books. There were a lot of them, but Mama said she knew which ones were good on account of her courses in psychology at the college. She talked about it in a very loud voice at the bookstore. "This one's no good . . . this one is . . ." "At Radcliffe we were very progressive." "This one . . . ha . . . ha! Definitely old hat!"

When we got home she started reading. She read and read and read. Finally she was ready and she and Daddy disappeared into their bedroom to set up.

At first it was kind of fun. They'd call us in one by one, and for ten, fifteen, twenty minutes, you'd have their total undivided attention. They'd ask you questions, and listen carefully to every word you said. "Um hum . . ." "Uh huh . . ." "That's very interesting . . . tell me more . . ." Mama did most of the interviewing. Daddy was more eager to get on with the inkblots and color tests. He'd lay the color tests all out on the bed. Large squares of colored cardboard.

"Choose one," he'd say, jingling the change in his blue jeans. "Choose one." I'd choose one and Mama would say "Ahh . . ." and write something down in her notebook.

"Choose another," Daddy would say. "Choose another." And I would until they were all gone.

Then it was inkblot time. You'd usually only have to do one or two of these. Daddy had little paper marks on the pages of the inkblot book so he could flip to the inkblot easily.

"What is it?" he'd say. And you'd stare at the black smudge and try to think of something interesting to say. You found out pretty quick that if you thought it was something ugly, like an old hag or something, not to say it. Otherwise you'd be in that bedroom forever.

Once I did real bad on my color test. Mama and Daddy decided I was "depressed, hostile and suicidal."

Everyone else was happy cause they got let off the hook for the rest of the weekend, while Mama and Daddy did a battery of tests and counseling sessions on me.

"Anna, do you know why you're here?" Daddy demanded.

"We are worried about you, Anna," said Mama, smoothing down my hair. "We are very, very concerned."

"Is there anything you would like to say, Anna? Anything you would like to share with us?" Daddy's face leans in close.

"Ummm . . . I love you?"

"Anna!" Daddy thunders. "That's not what we're talking about! You know what we're talking about!"

"I do?"

"Richard! Let me handle this! Anna, we love you very much, but you're going to have to stop resisting us. We are doing this for your own good." On and on this went. Interrupted only by breaks where I had to go outside and throw rocks at a tree, Daddy's idea. Or punch a pillow and scream. Mama's idea.

"Louder, Anna. Scream louder."

"Mama?" says Katie, her head poking around the door. "Mama, what's Anna doing?"

"Get out of here!" I scream. *"Get out!"* I run after her and throw the pillow. *"Out!"*

"Anna," says Mama in a smooth modulated voice, "Anna, it is good to get out your anger. But you must not misplace it. You must not transfer it to Katie. Deal with it. Release it . . . release it to the pillow."

"No!" I yell. *"No!"* And I run from her room.

"Anna!" I hear her call after me. But I don't stop. I run and run, my cheeks burning. Run and run until I am deep in the woods. Then I throw myself face down in the safety of the thick green moss.

The Charleston

I guess I feel partly to blame. I was asking Mama about the olden days. She told me about the Charleston, and flappers, and women taping their breasts down and things.

Somehow one thing had led to another and now Mama was showing me how it went.

165

"Let's see . . ." she said, looking kind of embarrassed. "Humm . . . It went kind of like this . . . ta . . . ta da dah da . . ." She started knocking her knees together and flapping her arms. She must have forgotten about taping her breasts down. Mama's gotten kind of fat, and one thing you can't say about her is that she has small breasts. Her breasts are *huge!* Well they were flopping up and down. Rising up to her shoulders and then slapping back down onto her stomach, making soft plopping noises.

When she stopped she was slightly out of breath. Mama is not in very good shape, I guess cause she's so fat. She's teaching first grade now, and her students are always asking her if she's pregnant. But she's not.

She started to sit down, tiny wisps of hair escaping from her bun. I saw Daddy was looking at her. Daddy doesn't look at Mama very much. Well I guess Mama must have noticed, cause she got a little smile in the corners of her mouth. And didn't sit down. Asked me if I wanted to see some more Charleston. But she wasn't talking to me, cause she was looking in Daddy's direction.

I said okay, but I felt funny in my stomach.

Mama started the Charleston again. Bigger this time. She started kicking her legs and stepping from side to side. Her breasts were really flopping now, making loud smacking noises. Her arms were flailing. She was singing loud. Real loud.

"Ta da dah ta ta!"

Daddy was laughing. She started giggling too. She thought he was laughing with her. But he was laughing at her.

She finally stopped. Her face was real red. There was sweat on her forehead and stains under her arms. She wasn't breathing good, but trying to pretend it was no effort at all.

She looked at me and said in triumph, "So *that's* the Charleston, Anna!" Then she looked back at Daddy expectantly.

He looked at her for a second and then went back to reading Charles Darwin's *On the Origin of Species*. Not a word. Not a single word.

She stood there awkward. Hair falling down.

I hated him.

Going to Church

We've started to go to church now. Not that Mama believes in God or anything, cause she doesn't. She believes in reincarnation. But we go to church anyway, cause Mama likes to sing.

She used to sing light opera in Boston. Mostly understudies and things but once she played the part of Patience. And when it came to the song about how a brother leaves a sister and the sobbing sister weeps, Mama would always weep! Real tears! Always at the same part of the song. Every night, like clockwork.

She's real proud of this. Told us over and over. How the tears glistened on her cheeks, the audience silent. How you could hear a pin drop when she was singing, so entranced were they, so moved.

One day Katie and I were rummaging in the basement, and we found a bunch of dusty old boxes. We opened one and it was filled with Mama's Radcliffe yearbooks. Mama was accepted at a lot of colleges, but she chose Radcliffe because it was right next door to Harvard. And so, not only were there going to be a lot of men close by, but there were going to be a lot of smart men. And since finding a husband was the reason her daddy sent her to college, she'd have a better chance of finding one there. Her daddy always used to say to her, "Jean, never think you're too good for a man. If someone wants to take you out, you go out and count your blessings."

I think he said this cause Grandmother thought she was too good for him.

"Marrying your grandfather was the worst mistake I ever made," she said to me that night I slept over. "And my god, look at the mess your mother has made of her life. Never get married, Anna. Never get married."

"I won't," I said. Cause I want her to like me.

So anyway, all of Granddaddy's "Find yourself a husband, Jean . . . Find yourself a husband . . ." didn't work, cause Mama was around all those Harvard men, and she still didn't have one. Graduated in the top ten percent at Radcliffe.

So she started singing in this opera company, and my daddy saw her singing one night and he asked her to marry him, so she did. They got divorced when Granddaddy died and left all his money to Grandmother and nothing for Mama. My daddy was mad, and threw her down and gave her a concussion and a broken arm. So Mama left him.

Anyway we found Mama's old yearbooks. We dusted them off and looked through them. Mama was real pretty. Had a diamond watch and pincurled hair and red, red lipstick. Belonged to a lot of sororities and glee clubs. Pictures of her in the symphony. "First flute!" she said proudly, tapping the picture with her finger. "First flute!"

We went through some more boxes and found her flute. She wiped it off with a real soft cloth, and started blowing on it. It didn't sound very good. Mama said she was out of practice. We dug into another box and found her old opera music books and records. Mama cleaned them all off, and we played opera. It was fun, we learned all the words and tunes and harmonies. And I guess all that singing going on made Mama decide to join the church.

So now we go to church.

At first us kids were pretty excited by the idea. A lot of our friends go to church. It's really in fashion. And when they'd talk about what happened, I'd feel a little left out.

But the part I didn't really count on was how boring it was. It was real real boring. You had to sit there for hours and hours listening to the minister talk. And he would talk on and on about all kinds of things that didn't make sense. And you weren't allowed to move. Had to sit there on that hard wood bench. Couldn't scratch. Even if you had a real bad itch, cause Mama said it would embarrass the family.

Easy for her to say. She had a nice comfortable chair right up there on the stage. And Mama would sit there, smiling beatifically, nodding her head up and down, murmuring intermittently, "Yes . . . yes!"

But the worst part was when she would get up to sing. She wouldn't sing like the other mothers. Oh no! Up she would spring. Pretending to be oh so modest and unassuming. Like it took some real arm twisting to get her up on that stage, and the next thing you know, she's blasting your eardrums off. Feet planted solid so the sound won't knock her over. Chins quivering, mouth opened wide. Really really wide, so you could practically see her tonsils. Loud singing. Loud! Loud! Loud!

I wanted to die. I just wished the earth would swallow me up right then and there.

The grown-ups would come up to us afterwards and say, "Oh you must be so proud . . ." "Your mother has such a lovely voice . . ." But I would just stare at my shoes, face stubborn, and not answer. Not answer, while Mama would waft around, beaming. Just beaming at everybody, smiling, nodding her head modestly, saying, "Oh thank you, thank you . . ." "You're so kind . . ."

And then we'd go home and she'd want to go over the event. Hash and rehash. Who wore what . . . Who said what . . . Who was sleeping with who . . .

The only good part about going to church was the money.

Mama always gave us kids ten cents or a quarter to put in the collection plate. And one day I caught Katie eating some candy. And I asked her where she got it, and she said she bought it. And I asked her where she got the money, and she told me that when the collection plate came around she kept the money Mama gave her and put a penny in instead. And when I said, "What about God?" She said, "What God? Besides if there is a God, He doesn't need money. If he wants something He can just make it."

So now after church, Katie and I go down to Mary's cafe and buy candy. We didn't tell anyone else though.

Cause if there were too many pennies in the collection plate the minister might get suspicious.

The Fight

Nick's gone. Got in a big fight with Daddy. Daddy caught him stealing a pack of his cigarettes, so he beat him up. Beat him up all the way from the living room to outside, halfway down the driveway.

Daddy beat him up real bad. Shoved him, kicked him, punched him. Punched him hard. Real hard. Nick had a bleeding face, but he just kept hitting Daddy back. Hitting him back and yelling. Yelling swear words. It was scary. Scary but exciting. Nice to see Daddy get hit back for a change.

So anyway, Nick ran away, and we don't get to see much of him anymore.

He's living on his own now. Down the road at the hippy commune. They're happy to have him, cause he's such a good hunter.

He dropped out of school and hunts full-time now.

Once in a while he'll drop by the school to make sure we're okay. Eating all right and stuff. Brings us deer meat sandwiches. Pats our heads kind of awkwardly and mutters,

"Now you just tell me if you need anything . . . Just let me know . . . You know where I'm staying, right? You just let me know." He tries to say it all casual like, but his face gets all pale and concerned. "Anything, anything at all. Richard treating you okay? He hurts you, you let me know."

He's kind of a hero at school. I guess on account of his dropping out, and living on his own and everything.

He has a lot of girlfriends now.

Mama's Vacation

Mama was having real bad asthma, so why she decided it was the day to clean the house, I don't know.

Mama doesn't clean the house very often. Us kids are in charge of all that. But every once in a while she gets real angry and starts bustling. I decided when Mama's bustling, to stay out of her way. The last time I offered to help, I was held up as an example. Good Anna, thoughtful Anna, kind and considerate Anna. And then spent the rest of the day cleaning and listening to a tirade against my selfish, evil, wicked, greedy brothers and sisters. She always does this. It drives me crazy. Then she sat me down and forced me to eat a big bowl of chocolate chip ice cream in front of my brothers and sisters. She told them I got ice cream cause I'm good, and they didn't cause they're bad.

So I don't offer to help. I hid upstairs with my sisters, and laughed at Mama with her martyrish way, flushed face and wheezing heaving chest. I laughed and felt guilty.

Later Mama staggered to the Volkswagen. "Where are you going, Mama?" I asked. She waved her hands futilely in the air, as if to fend off the question. Face blotchy, dark ringed eyes puffed up from crying. Bluish green around her nose and mouth. She slowly gets in the car. Gasping for breath. Fumbling with the key. I watch, panic growing. "Where are you going, Mama?" I ask again. Tears catch and form little steamy pools at the bottom of her glasses. The key finds the hole. The car catches and she slowly haltingly reverses the car and drives away . . .

"Where are you going, Mama?" I yell. I yell it and yell it until the car disappears, leaving only a trail of dust . . . But she doesn't answer.

Mama's in the hospital. Daddy took us to see her. He didn't go up though. He stayed in the parking lot because, as I've mentioned before, he doesn't believe in doctors.

We went up. Tiptoed into her room. Quiet.

Mama was lying on the bed, tubes coming out of her arm, a white plastic bracelet with her name and a lot of confusing numbers on it. I'd never seen Mama look so happy. I guess it must be nice to be in the hospital and have everybody pay you so much attention.

The nurses came in and looked at us kids and then shook their heads, tsking and clucking, "All those children . . . Oh you poor little thing." Mama laughed her gay little social laugh, pretending it was nothing, and then she dissolved into a wheezing, crumpled heap. Baby Will started crying. Susan tried to pick him up and make him feel better. But it didn't work, only made him scream louder. Scream louder and kick and punch, and arch his body. So Susan put him down and he ran over to Mama and tried to climb up on her. The nurses told us to go home. So we did.

Daddy didn't ask us about Mama, and when we talked about her, he changed the subject.

I curled up on the sofa in the living room and started reading *Emily of the New Moon* for the millionth time. I love that old brown sofa. The fabric was pretty skinny, and you had to be careful where you sat, cause one of the springs was poking through on the other side, but even so, it was the best reading place in the house. The good side was soft, and it was always warm, cause of the sunshine through the window. Even on cloudy days I'd manage to capture a few brief bursts of sunlight. It made me feel like a cat. You know how cats always sit in windows. Curled up and cozy, gobbling up the sunshine. That was me! Anna the cat, curled up on the sofa, reading, gobbling up the sunshine.

Susan was cooking dinner in the kitchen. Chicken fricassee! It smelled *good!* I was hungry, but then again, I'm always hungry. I think the only thing better than eating, is waiting to eat, waiting to eat something delicious. You know you're going to eat, so you don't have to panic, you can just sit there and let your mouth get hungrier.

"Anna, come here." I looked up. Daddy was sitting in his black vinyl chair smoking, smiling at me with his false teeth. "Come here and make it snow." I hate doing this, but Daddy was in a funny mood, and I didn't want to make him mad. So I scratched his head and watched the dead grayish flakes of scalp fall, covering the shoulder of the chair. Susan walked by. I guess she had to get something upstairs. Well anyway, he grabbed her. He grabbed her, pulled her onto his lap, laughing. Tickling her. Yelling, "You can't get away!" over and over, laughing. Laughing loud. Susan was laughing too, but I could tell she was scared. I was scared too. My tummy was feeling real funny, but I just kept scratching his head. Then Daddy stopped laughing, well he didn't stop really, but it was different. Kind of more like a giggling sound. High-pitched, nervous, scared or something. Then I saw his hand moving . . . His left arm wrapped around her, gripping her hard. His right hand moving, tickling, jerky, tickling, pulling up her skirt, tickling, tickling, down, down into her panties. Pulling, tugging, clumsy, ripping. Sweating, him sweating and breathing hard. Susan struggling, crying. Me frozen. Couldn't breathe, couldn't move, couldn't speak. Eyes stuck, glued to his hand, his hand tickling where Susan's pee comes out. Nobody was laughing now, not even Daddy. Then all of a sudden I grabbed his arm. Grabbed his arm and pulled. Pulled hard. Laughing. Tickling, pulling, laughing, scratching. Scared, so scared, pretending it was a game. Then, we're all laughing. Laughing so hard it hurts my ears. And Daddy lets go, looking kinda strange, like his throat wants to cry. But we don't look back. We run. We run upstairs to my bedroom, climb out the window and crawl onto the roof. Daddy can't get up there. We don't talk about it. We sit there on the roof and sing. Every once in a while Daddy tries to get us to come down. Tells us dinner is burning . . . That he'll be good, won't be bad anymore. But we don't answer. Ignore him. Just sing louder until he goes away.

It's a beautiful sunset.

When it's dark, and the house is quiet, we crawl off the roof, and go to bed.

Kissing Lessons

Daddy came upstairs last night. It was "time for kissing lessons," he said. He was naked. He practiced lots and lots, more with Susan though. Acting like it was just a casual sort of thing, you know, the way other daddies teach their kids baseball or fishing. But he didn't fool us. We knew what he was about.

"Open your lips, don't keep them tight. Soft, they must be soft." But I pretended I didn't understand and kept them clenched shut tight. "No, your lips must be open like this so our tongues can touch. The tongues must kiss. This is french kissing, this is the way grown-ups kiss."

I wanted to be a grown-up, but there was no way his slimy tongue was going in my mouth!

After our kissing lessons were over, he lay on the bed, squished in between us, and talked about when he and Mama first met. "It was nineteen fifty-five. Your mama was still going to her highfalutin university. She was sitting on the lawn in front of the library and I said to myself, 'That girl has Richard Smith written all over her.' I asked her out a few times, but she always said no. Thought she was too good for me. And then, lo and behold, ten years later, almost to the day. Who should I run into, but your mama! Absolutely by chance. I was watching my friend's art gallery. Andre, you remember Andre. Anyway, he had to make a delivery across town, so I was watching the place and then who should walk in but your mama! It was raining and she had come in to get out of the rain. Her red dress was soaking wet, clinging to her body. She was shivering and I could see her nipples. 'Jean,' I said. 'Jean Henley . . .' She looked up, our eyes met, and the rest is history."

I wanted to shift my body, but I didn't want to remind him I was there. So I stayed were I was, didn't move. Stayed suffocating in his smelly armpit.

"Yes, your mama, with all her airs. All her airs and finery. Well let me tell you something, she's not so prim and proper in bed. She's a little wildcat. Makes me tie her up and spank her." He laughs and rubs us in closer. "Yes sir, a regular little wildcat! You want to know how we spent our honeymoon? You want to know what your mama made me do? Made me take her to strip shows! Strip shows, peep shows, porn movies. Anything with sex in it! The more sex the better!" Then he let go of me and rolled on top of Susan, wiggling his hips back and forth. He tried to pull her blanket down, but she kept it on her tight. "Susan, Susan baby, why don't you come downstairs. I have a book down there. A book you might find interesting. A grown-up book. Why don't you come downstairs?"

"No," Susan whispered. "No, I don't want to."

"Why?" said Daddy, rubbing his hands up and down her body. "Why? You might find it enlightening." Daddy lying there, rubbing her all over with his repulsive body.

"I don't believe you!" I said in a disgusted voice. "I don't believe you about Mama!"

"Well it's true."

"Well I don't believe you. I think you're lying."

"Anna!"

"And I guess," I continued, "the only way to find out is to ask Mama! Right, Susan?"

"Yeah . . . we'll ask Mama."

Well Daddy thought about that for a little while and then he decided to go back downstairs. Susan started crying. She was real scared. Said over and over again, "Don't leave me alone with Daddy . . . Don't leave me alone with Daddy."

And I said I wouldn't. I promised . . . And I won't. I never will as long as I live.

*C*ocoon *K*eeper

*W*e lie in my bed and wait. Moist, damp, wet under our clothes. Blankets wrapped around us tight, like a cocoon. Waiting, throats tight, hearts beating too loud. Waiting, listening, eyes open, tracing the cracks in the ceiling, holding hands, tight, clenched. Then we hear it. Mama and Daddy's bedroom door squeak open. His footsteps, *creak* . . .

creak . . . Up the stairs, nine stairs. We lie there, ice cold under our clothes. Lots of clothes, even though it's summer. Frozen under our turtlenecks, sweaters, tights, pants and dresses. Hands sweat and slip, grasp even tighter.

Susan's bedroom door creaks open. "Susan . . ." he whispers, "Susan," rummaging in her bed. But she's not there! Oh no, she's safe with me. Wrapped tight, with our blankets. We hear him swear under his breath. Then he's back in the hall again. Outside my door.

We force shut our eyes, still our bodies, heads, hearts pounding, exploding.

The door opens slow, so slow. I can feel him standing, looking at me, frowning. Sweat trickling, tickling, making my body need to squirm. Hair damp to my face. My mouth tastes of salt, salt and dust.

I feel him come over to the bed. I can smell him now. Susan tightens her grip on my hand. Trying to control her raggity breath. "Susan," he whispers. I hear him move, crouch down beside her. I squint my eyes and watch him through my eyelashes. He is stroking her hair. "Susan baby, come downstairs . . . I'm lonely . . . I'm so lonely without your mama."

Kissing her now on the mouth, Susan pretending to be asleep, but I can see the tears sliding out of her shut eyes.

He tries to pick her up and carry her, but he can't cause the blankets are wound around and around and around us.

Then I sit up and yell loud, really loud. *"What's going on here!"* Scared, heart racing, face ready to be hit.

He looks at me, trapped, caught.

Quickly I flop back down and wrap my arms and legs

around her, hold my breath, pretend to go to sleep. I watch him through my eyelashes, kneeling there awkward. Susan trembling underneath me. But he doesn't go away, and he doesn't go away. So I scrunch up my eyes and try to sound casual, sleepy. "Go away, Daddy, we're trying to sleep."

So he stands up slowly and lets go of Susan and goes back downstairs.

Finally Susan sleeps and I watch over her. Hot and scratchy. I keep the mosquitoes away and listen to Daddy cry in his bedroom.

Buckerfield's

We were taking the ferry to the mainland to get groceries. Susan and I got dressed up cause we were going to town. But that was a mistake, cause Daddy thought we were wearing dresses for him.

"Shouldn't wear clothes like that. Just asking for trouble," he said, looking Susan up and down.

When we get to town he drives to Safeway. Hands me some money, tells me to get out, he and Susan are going to Buckerfield's to pick up some chicken feed and I'm supposed to get the groceries. But I look at Susan all scared and stiff and I say, "No."

"What?" says Daddy. "I don't think I heard you properly."

"No," I say. And then I try to make it light, like a joke or something. "I want to go to Buckerfield's, Daddy. I want to go with you."

I smile at him, but he's not smiling back.

"Get out, you brat!"

"No," I say, still smiling. "I want to go to Buckerfield's."

His face turns all red and he hits me and hits me over and over in the face. But I keep yelling, "No! I want to go to Buckerfield's! I want to go to Buckerfield's!"

Susan is crying and saying, "Stop . . . Stop . . ." But he doesn't. Then he grabs me by my arm and the back of my dress, yanks the van door open, throws me out, and drives away. Drives away fast. I get up, my knees are scraped up pretty bad. I run after the van yelling, "I want to go to Buckerfield's!" But I can't catch up. He's driving too fast.

I buy the groceries. I keep my head down. I'm crying and people are looking but I don't care. I can't help it.

I sit on the curb outside of Safeway with the groceries. Everything's defrosting. The sun is setting.

Finally the van comes. Susan's been crying. Daddy looks jaunty. Happy even. He has scratches on his face.

"Here, sweetheart," he says to Susan. "Get yourself some new underwear. Pretty ones!" He hands her some money. A twenty-dollar bill. Then he hands her another five and says, "And get your mama a pair too. She'll like that."

Susan goes into Field's. I run after her, but she won't

look at me or speak to me. She buys the underwear and we go home.

Mama's Return

Susan won't talk to me. Talk to me or look at me. Walks around all stiff-legged. Sleeps in her own room and Daddy visits her.

"When Mama gets back," I tell myself. "When Mama gets back," I say over and over. "She'll make everything okay. Take away Susan's stiff-legged walk, her ashamed eyes. Take away her swollen, pale face. Her bruised lips." I cry myself to sleep. "When Mama gets back . . . when Mama gets back."

Finally the hospital lets her come home.

"You must not bother your mama," Daddy says. "She has been very, very sick. She needs to rest if she is to get better. You must not bother her." He sticks close to Mama. Is very attentive. Doesn't let me get near. But one day he's gone. Goes to the post office. I hide in Katie's closet until he leaves so he can't make me go with him. He calls and calls but I don't answer. Then I go downstairs. Stand outside Mama's bedroom, heart pounding. I take a big breath and tap on the door. Tap on it soft so as not to disturb her. "Mama?" She doesn't answer, but I have to go on, don't have much time. I tap again, a little harder this time. "Mama? Mama, are you awake?" Her voice comes out all sleepy like. "Yes, Anna, what is it?"

"Can I come in?"

"Sure honey, come on in."

I open the door and slip inside, shut the door fast so no one can see me go in.

Mama smiles at me. "I missed you when I was at the hospital."

"I missed you too," I say. The words barely creeping out of my mouth. "I really missed you . . ." And I start to cry.

Mama sits up and opens up her arms and I crawl into the safety of them. Curl up into a little tiny ball and Mama strokes my hair. And the bursting that was trapped in my chest for so long unravels itself.

"Mama . . . Mama . . . I missed you . . . I missed you . . . I didn't know what to do, Mama . . . I didn't know what to do." I cling to her, I cling to her like a person drowning. "I didn't know what to do."

"To do about what, Anna? To do about what?"

I feel her body going tense beneath me but I can't stop it now, it comes out like a runaway train. "Daddy . . . Daddy hurt Susan. He hurt her bad. I tried to stop him, Mama, I tried to stop him." I am crying so hard I am choking on my spit. "But I couldn't, Mama . . . I couldn't."

"Wait!" Mama says. "Wait!" And she pushes me away. Pushes me away almost angrily. She grabs her glasses from the bedside table and puts them on. "What are you talking about!" She is glaring at me, her cheeks two bright red patches.

"What are you talking about!" she demands. And I feel confused, guilty, like I've done something wrong.

"He . . . he . . . hurt her." My words stumble, falter. "Daddy . . . hurt her . . ." My voice fades to a whisper.

Mama makes a noise. A noise rising up from her belly, rising up to be trapped in the back of her throat. *"Nnnaghh!!"* she goes, and I think she is going to hit me. Then she flings back her blanket, grabs her robe and wraps it around her as she storms up the stairs.

"Susan!" she yells. *"Susan!"*

"Yes, Mama," says Susan. And Mama marches into Susan's room and slams the door.

I hear Mama's voice rising and falling like hailstones around Susan's head. I hear Susan crying. Crying and crying. And I stand at the foot of the stairs shaking. My whole body shaking like I'm sitting on a washing machine on spin. Then Mama comes out. Comes out of Susan's room. Gripped in her fist is a scrap of pale blue material. When she gets closer I can see the dried-up blood on it. And I know it is Susan's undies from Buckerfield's. Mama doesn't look at me. It's as if I don't exist. She bumps past me, staggers to her bed and falls onto it. A low moan starting up, and another and another. All curled up, rocking back and forth, Susan's undies clutched to her chest.

Richard

Richard. That's what I'm calling him now. Richard. I can tell he doesn't like it, but there's nothing he can do about it, after all that's his name. And he's not my daddy, never will be. He stinks, has big feet and hurt Susan. And I hate him.

I'm not supposed to talk about it, so I won't. But I hate him. I hate him and I will never forgive him.

I'm mad at Mama too. Somehow I thought when I told her what had happened, things would change. But nothing did really. Oh, little things perhaps. After I told her, he slept in the basement. And there were these little oval things in the medicine cabinet. Things that Susan was supposed to stick inside of her after he hurt her, so she wouldn't get pregnant.

But basically, that was it.

He kept on hurting Susan, and Mama kept on pretending nothing was happening.

Sleep

I keep having this same dream over and over again.

I am bouncing a ball, a small rubber ball on the cement. It seems innocent enough, but it isn't. I must not stop bouncing the ball. There is one person standing, staring at me, whispering. Every time I bounce the ball it grows bigger, and there is another person standing there staring at me whispering. The ball grows and grows, the crowd grows and grows and gets louder and louder. I can't stop bouncing the ball. It is huge. By now the crowd is yelling, screaming, crashing in my ears. They're close. Surrounding me. I'm trapped. Can't breathe. Panic. No hope. Nowhere to turn. Alone, I'm so alone. Crying, I am crying and bouncing the ball, bouncing the ball that is bigger than me. The crowd louder and louder. Then all of a sudden the ball starts to get smaller, the crowd melts away, until finally there is only me again, bouncing the ball, the small rubber ball on the cement. There is only one person standing, staring, whispering, but there is no relief in this. I can't relax, I know it will only start up again. And it does. Bigger, more, bigger, more, bigger, more, yelling, yelling. Softer, less, softer, less, softer, less, just me bouncing, bouncing the ball . . . It goes on and on until I wake up.

I wake up downstairs in Mama's arms. I am crying, crying. Can't stop. Mama strokes my hair and holds me. "Shhh . . . Anna . . . shhh . . . It's okay, honey . . . It's okay . . . shh . . . shhh . . . It's only a dream . . . only a dream."

Stale Air

Richard's still living in the basement. He's brought his black vinyl armchair and Mama's old typewriter down. Why? you might ask. Why the typewriter? Well, Richard has decided to write a novel. Richard who hasn't even finished high school has now decided he is a novelist. And what is his novel about? Himself of course, and how he is the second coming of Christ. I kid you not. He actually believes it.

So now the basement doesn't just smell of musty old things and mildew. It smells of Richard. It stinks. I have to hold my breath, and breathe big gulps of air outside the basement door when I go down. And unfortunately, I have to go down there a lot. I'm on double laundry duty because Mama doesn't want Susan down in the basement. And I hate it. I really do, cause I have this thing about breathing Richard's air. I know it might sound weird, but it feels as if he's breathed up all the oxygen, and just left waste and poison for me. Not only that, but like I said before, he stinks. If you blindfolded me and took me into a room where he had been, I would know it.

The smell of stale cigarettes, unwashed body, dandruff . . . You might think it's strange for me to say dandruff. You might say, "How can you smell dandruff?" Well I tell you I can. It has a very distinct pungent oily smell. And I should know too, cause I've had to scratch his head often enough. It takes me forever and a lot of soap to get the smell off my hands and out of my nails.

So as you can imagine, if you're trapped in the basement doing laundry, and he's living there, smoking, typing his "great novel" with two fingers, and red-rimmed eyes . . . breathing all the air, it's bound to be a little suffocating.

Every once in a while he takes one of the guns and goes out in the woods. He always makes a big show of it. Trying to make us feel sorry for him. Pretending he's going to kill himself. He always wants one of us kids to run after him, grab his arm, try to talk him out of it. Joy's done it a few times, Katie too. But I never do. I just watch him go. Standing silent. Praying that he will . . . But he never does. He always comes back a couple of hours later. Eyes red and swollen, shoulders bowed, shivering from the cold. Sneaks back. Trying to slip inside unnoticed. But I don't let him. I go downstairs and bang around with the laundry. He used to try to talk to me. Ask me questions about school, Susan, Baby Will. But I wouldn't answer.

Then one day, after his usual romp in the woods, in he crept. Sat on his mattress, gun in his arms. Gun in his arms trying to look oh so pathetic, and I got mad. "Why don't you just do it," I said as I jammed the dirty clothes into the washing machine. "Why don't you just do it." I started up the washing machine, turned around and glared at him. "Well?" He stared at me for a moment, didn't answer, then he put the gun down, eyes slipping away.

So now he doesn't try to talk to me and I don't talk to him. Just ignore him and send him my hate waves.

Applesauce

We have this great hill for sledding. Steep! Straight down, and I mean *straight!* What I do is take a running start to get maximum speed, then right before I hit the edge, I hold my sled real tight and fling my belly up onto it, and dive face first down the hill. I'm really daring too, really hurl myself down. Dodging bushes, big rocks, trees. Wind, snow, ice chips flying. Breakneck speed. Soaring, sailing, careening, crashing, falling tumbling over and over.

The goal? The creek! Haven't reached it yet . . . But I will.

Before school I practice. After school I run all the way home from the bus stop. Do my chores as fast as I can. Then I practice until it gets dark. I practice and practice. I will reach it yet.

Anyway, I was practicing when I heard this yelling. At first I thought it was just the wind in my ears, but when my sled finally stopped I could still hear it. High-pitched and frantic. "Will's gone! Baby Will's gone!" Wailing, shrieking, more voices joining in. I scrambled back up the hill. At the top I could see everyone running around. Crying and crying and calling, "Will! Will!"

I wanted to say something, ask what happened. But my voice wouldn't seem to come out, I just stood there hugging my frozen sled.

Then Mama ran up to me, grabbed me by the shoulders and shook me. "Anna! Anna! Have you seen Will?"

"No, Mama."

"Think! Think! Are you sure?" She was still shaking me. Shaking me hard, like she thought I'd swallowed him and if she shook me hard enough she'd shake him out.

"Yes, Mama," I said. "Yes I'm sure." She gave me another shake. "Well then what are you standing around here for? Go then! Go look!" Then she yelled over her shoulder to no one in particular. "Nobody stops until we find him!"

We looked and we looked. We looked in the creek, the woods, the barn, the chicken house . . . everywhere. But we couldn't find him.

It got darker and darker, the cold deeper and deeper, couldn't stop shaking, stomach hungry, head hurting, and still we couldn't find him.

Finally Mama called us in, her eyes all puffy, and we had peanut butter sandwiches and went to bed. Richard went into Mama's bedroom and I could hear them making moaning, bumping noises late into the night.

When we woke, Mama called in sick. "No school today," she said, Richard holding her close. "No school today, we have to find Will."

So we got dressed really warm and went back outside to look.

Around one o'clock, the neighbor Berta De Pont came

running up the hill. She can't speak any English, only Spanish, cause she comes from Mexico. And her husband Louis can only speak French cause he comes from Quebec. But they fell in love, so they got married. Anyway, she came running up the hill and told Mama in Spanish that there was a phone call for Mama, and Mama understood her cause she took Spanish at Radcliffe, so Mama went running back down the hill with her, both yelling in Spanish at the top of their lungs.

When Mama got back she called a family conference. Baby Will had been found. A neighbor found him yesterday. The problem was, the neighbor refused to give him back. Said she just called because she had heard that we were worried and she wanted to let us know that he was safe. But that she wouldn't let us have him back, because Mama was a bad mother and didn't deserve him. Not only that but she had a shotgun, so Mama shouldn't even bother to try to go and get him cause she'd probably get shot. So then it was decided that I should go instead. Cause I'm the best in emergencies. Like the time we had that chimney fire. I woke up, smelled smoke and started screaming, *"Fire! Fire!"* Real loud. Woke everybody up. Then I grabbed Baby Will, wrapped his blanket around him so he wouldn't get cold and ran outside. Didn't even put my shoes on. Remembered the story Mama told us about this bathhouse in San Francisco burned down, and how the only person to survive was this one man who ran out stark naked. Didn't stop to put on his clothes like everyone else. Just ran out stark naked into the streets of San Francisco.

I got dressed in my good clothes and brushed my hair.

Mama and Richard drove me to the neighbor's driveway. And then they left. They would have driven me farther, but they were kind of nervous about the lady with the shotgun. And they didn't know how long or short the driveway was.

I started walking. It was long! Real long, and uphill too! I had to take several breaks, cause the backs of my legs were burning up, also I was a bit scared cause of her threats about shooting and stuff.

Finally I could see the house. It was brown with green trim. Neat, tidy. I approached it cautiously, didn't see any guns . . . Then a man came around the corner, not too tall, gray hair sort of greasy but not in a bad way, kind eyes, stooped shoulders. He looked surprised to see me and he didn't have a gun.

"Yes?" he said in a gentle voice. "Can I help you?"

"I've come for my brother," I said more boldly than I felt.

"Oh," he said, nodding his head thoughtfully. Then he sat down on a stump used for splitting wood. "Well," he said finally, "I guess you'll have to talk to my wife about that." He got up slowly, sort of reluctant like, and offered me his arm. "Come on," he said. And then he kind of half chuckled, patted my hand and said, "Don't look so worried, she won't bite."

The house was warm inside, a wood stove burning, the smells of homebaked foods and canning. A large hooked rug on the floor, a clock ticking. "Martha," he called. "There's someone here to see you . . . She's come for her brother."

Nobody came.

He yelled, "Martha," but she still didn't come. So he said, "Excuse me please," and went into the kitchen. I could hear the soft rumble of their voices.

Finally they came into the room. His arm was around her. Supporting her. She was soft. Soft gray hair, soft curves, a dress soft and worn from many washings.

"She can't have him," she said, eyes dark. "She can't! He could have died out there! Died! She doesn't deserve him." And tears started welling up in her eyes. "She can't have him! She can't! He was naked! Naked! Just standing out there stark naked, wearing one red boot, that's all. One red boot, holding the other, crying and crying. Stark naked in all that snow! She can't have him! She can't! It's just not fair!"

Her husband turned her to him and hugged her, stroking her hair, clumsy but gentle. "It's all right, Martha . . . It's okay . . . I love you, it's okay . . ."

When she stopped crying he got her a Kleenex and she blew her nose and stuck it in the pocket of her apron.

He sat her down on the sofa, arm still around her.

"Martha," he said. "You know we can't keep him."

"Why not?" she said, her body limp, looking down at her hands. "She has so many."

"We can't, that's all, we just can't."

The clock ticked, the fire crackled, and they were quiet. Him holding her. Finally she said, "Well, she'll have to wait, because the baby's asleep and I'm not going to wake him." The man let his breath out and she got up and went into the kitchen and blew her nose again.

The man asked me if I'd like an apple, and I said, "Okay," cause I was real hungry. So we went outside to the cellar to get one.

It was dark, and fragrant-smelling. There was a whole bunch of apples piled up against the wall. It took a while to choose one, cause a lot had worm holes, but I have lots of experience with apples, so I found a good one. It had a bit of waxy stuff or oil or something on it, so I rubbed it on my coat. It was kind of soft and mushy cause it was so old, but it had a real good flavor.

We stayed outside until I finished the apple cause he said she needed a bit of time. Didn't talk much. Didn't need to. Just sat outside on an old wooden bench. Sat there side by side, me nibbling my apple. Nibbling it slowly to make it last.

Baby Will was awake when we got back and he was real happy to see me. He wiggled out of her arms and toddled right over and gave me a big hug around my legs. Made my tummy warm.

She went into the kitchen and started bustling around again. Came out with a big jar of applesauce. Said she made it for him, so we might as well take it.

Made her husband drive us home. Made me promise to "bring Baby to visit . . . gets so lonely up here," she said. "Promise now." I promised, but Mama wouldn't let me.

Five

Field Trip

Lynn's grandmother lived in Seattle. So when our school went there for a field trip Lynn got to stay with her. I wasn't going to be able to go, cause I didn't have any relatives in Seattle, and my family couldn't afford all that extra money for the youth hostel. *But* . . . Lynn asked her grandmother if I could stay with her, and her grandmother said it was okay, so not only did I get to go to Seattle, but I also got to stay with Lynn. And the very best part of all was . . . *no* chaperones! We'd be able to go where we liked, do what we liked, without a how do you do to anybody! All the kids at school were real jealous!

Lynn's grandmother lived in an apartment on the fifth floor. She smoked all the time, never stopped. So the air was always hazy. Hazy and gray. Didn't talk much. Made food and slopped it on the table. She didn't eat. Just sat at the table and read magazines. Smoking her cigarettes, blowing the smoke right in our faces.

We weren't allowed to talk at the table, but when she wasn't looking, we'd make faces at Lynn's brother Robbie and try to make him crack up.

Robbie was in Susan's grade. He was actually quite obnoxious. Nobody liked him. Brian Thomason once took off all of Robbie's clothes and hung him by his underwear to the flagpole. Everybody laughed. And if you ever walked by a locker and you heard a banging or yelling from inside, you could be pretty sure it was Robbie. It hurt my stomach, but I figured he asked for it, cause he always acted like a real jerk.

Anyway, Lynn and me were making faces at him, trying to get him to crack up and get in trouble. And then I made a real funny face, just as he was taking a drink of milk, and the next thing you knew milk was everywhere, coming out of his nose, his mouth, spraying all over the table. It looked real funny and we couldn't help it, we just all started laughing right out loud, even Robbie, and their grandmother looked up from her magazine and whacked Robbie across the side of the head. Got him in trouble. But he didn't mind. Didn't even get mad at me. Told me I was a spunky little twerp.

That night when we were in bed we talked about all kinds of things. Things we'd never talked about before. Lynn told me how her dad used to beat up Robbie real bad. And how Robbie had scars all over his body cause when he was a little baby her dad used to put out his cigarette butts on him.

She told me she hated her dad and never saw him. Told me he lived here in Seattle but she wasn't going to see him cause of the things he'd done. And then she cried. I'd never seen Lynn cry before. I'd always thought her life was perfect, but here she was, crying quiet, body shaking in her fancy pink pajamas her mom had sewn up for her.

The next day we had the morning free. Had to meet up with our class at three in front of the planetarium. So we went to Marshall's and Lynn taught me how to steal. She said she'd done it before, but I don't know . . . I kinda think she was just saying that. Cause she was acting awful nervous.

Anyway, we went to Marshall's and bought a big shopping bag. It cost a quarter. Then we went downstairs. That's where the kid section is. And we tried on a whole bunch of tops. Narrowed it down to three each. Matching ones, cause we're best friends. Then we put two in our bag and bought one.

The saleslady was real nice. Kinda frazzled, middle-aged and dumpy, but nice. You could tell she thought we were cute, shopping all by ourselves. She kept saying, "My what big girls, shopping by yourselves . . ."

It was pretty funny. We laughed for a long time about that.

Riding back home on the school bus, Lynn let it drop, oh so casual, about what we did at Marshall's. Excitement in my belly. I felt different. Like a different person, you know. Kids looked at me different. Kinda a mixture of respect, awe, and a little scared. Nobody else in our class had ever stolen before. We were the first. I liked that.

Stealing gave me a rush. Made me feel strong, smart. Real smart. Outwit 'em all.

Another thing I discovered on the bus was if I scooted to the very edge of the seat with my bum, held on to the seat in front of me for balance, and stretched my toes way down, I could make my feet touch the floor while I was still sitting!

I told Lynn about it, and we sat that way until our muscles got sore.

Spaghetti Dinner

Mama and Richard have made some new friends. The Gordons. One of the teachers at Mama's school was having a housewarming party. Mama and Richard went. They have this new thing. They have decided to socialize more. Become part of the community. So they went to this thing and met Mr. and Mrs. Gordon. After the party they brought them over to our house. Swung by the Gordons' house first and picked up their kids. They were boring. I don't know why grown-ups always insist you like their friends' kids. Anyway, they came over and bored the hell out of us and then invited us over to their house Sunday for spaghetti dinner. Mama and Richard seemed real excited about the idea of going over there for dinner. But right before we left they got in a fight and Richard decided not to come. Sulking I guess. Mama was mad. But no matter what she said, he wouldn't come. Finally she herded all us kids into the car and did the old "All right then, I'm leaving without you." It didn't work though, cause he didn't come running after the car crying saying he'd be good like us kids do. Mama drove away real slowly until the house was out of sight.

Katie and Joy were arguing in the back. Not a bad argument, just a habit one, when all of a sudden Mama slammed on the brakes and screamed, "Enough! Enough! *Enough!*" Stopped so fast Susan banged her head on the back of Mama's seat. But Mama didn't notice, just sat there and cried. She cried and cried. Hitting the steering wheel over and over.

When she took off again she drove fast. Faster than I'd ever seen Mama drive before. Nobody said a word the whole way there. When we were almost at the Gordons' house Mama pulled the car over, blew her nose, took some asthma medicine and powdered her face.

We got there, and I must say, I was amazed. If I hadn't been in the car, I would have sworn nothing was wrong. Nothing. "Richard was working on his novel and couldn't be torn away!" Mama said, laughing gaily. Then she wafted over to the kitchen and poured herself a glass of red wine.

I went out in the yard. It was small with a picket fence around it. Half a picket fence really. The rest was kind of broken and fallen down. It had flecks of grayish white paint on it. There were some plants but they were dead. The ground was dry. Dry and dusty. I picked up a stick and started making patterns in the dirt. The most satisfying thing about doing this was the erasing. I'd draw and draw and draw with my stick, and then I'd drop down on my knees and erase and erase. Patting and smoothing my hands in the warm dust until not a trace was left. Then I'd pick up my stick and draw again.

I could smell the spaghetti sauce cooking, my stomach hungry. I wanted to go in and sneak a taste, but I couldn't face Mama. Mama being social and drinking too much wine. So I stayed outside.

After a while I got tired of drawing and erasing. I was feeling cold so I found a patch of sunlight around the side of the house. I scrunched up in it. The house was warm from the sun. I could feel the flaking paint rough on my back through my shirt.

Suddenly I heard a car start up. "Mama!" I yelled. I could hear it driving away. I ran around to the front of the house but I was too late, the car was already gone. "Mama!" I yelled. It came out again, "Mama!" I couldn't help it. I stood there dusty, clench-fisted.

The front door opened, I could hear it, feel someone looking. I didn't turn around, didn't want anyone to see I'd been crying. Then I heard Mama's voice. I turned around and there she was, standing in the doorway, a glass of wine clutched in her hand. "Come here, Anna," she said. I wiped my face with the back of my hand and went over, relief and loathing mixed. She put her arm around me and leaned in close, like she needed a hug. "Who left?" I asked. "Betty Lou . . ." Mama paused and then started laughing. "She seemed to think she'd have better luck convincing your father than I did!" Mama laughed again. We walked into the living room, her arm close around me, her sweat . . . desperation . . . red wine . . . I couldn't breathe.

Mrs. Gordon was gone for a long time. A very long

time. Finally I heard her car drive up. I ran outside and crouched behind a bush. I watched her get out of her car. She was hesitant, flushed, mussy. Then I stood up and yelled, *"Is he coming?"* She jumped a little, which was good. Then she walked over, hips swaying, she wasn't wearing her bra anymore. Her lips bruised. "He's following in his car," she said lightly, eyes bright, and then patted me on the head. I didn't say anything. I just looked at her. She thought she was fooling me but she wasn't. I could smell him all over her. All over. She should have taken a bath before she came back.

When Richard came everybody tried to act like nothing happened. They all talked, laughed, ate spaghetti, drank wine. So did I. Lots of wine. Five cupfuls. It made me kind of dizzy so Lenny said I could lie down in his room. But Richard and Mrs. Gordon were already in there. She was standing in the middle of the room in her pale peach slip. One of its straps had fallen off her shoulder. Richard was on his knees. His arms were around her . . . moving . . . pushing . . . Pushing her slip, her silk peach slip up over her hips. His face buried in her. Her head thrown back. Short black curls tousled. Her hands holding his head, stroking his hair, "Richard . . . Richard . . ." she was saying. I felt dizzy. The room swayed. I needed some fresh air. As I left I heard her say, "Oh my god, Richard! Anna!" Then she started calling me, "Anna! Anna! Come back! I can explain . . ." She started to cry but I didn't turn around. I needed some air. I went outside. It was real cold now. Lots of stars. Real cold. I ran. I ran and I ran.

When I got back Mama and Mr. Gordon were sitting silent in the living room. There were a lot of broken dishes in the fireplace.

Mama said it was time to go, so we all piled into the car and drove home.

Sasquatch Days

It's Sasquatch Days! Pretty much the highlight of the year as far as the island is concerned. Perfectly situated too. August fifteenth. Nice and warm. Just far enough into the summer for everyone to be good and bored. And since there's nothing else to do, you know everybody is going to be there! What to wear is a big issue.

Lynn's mom is a seamstress. So anytime Lynn sees something in a catalog, her mom just whips it up for her. Her family is the best dressed on the island.

Once when I was staying overnight, Lynn's mom was making swimming suits for Lynn and Julie. And she had some fabric left over, so she made one for me! A bikini, just like Lynn's, and we looked like twins. Not identical twins, cause she has blond hair and mine's dark brown. But we both have long hair down to our waist, and we're both skinny and almost the same height. She's three-quarters of an inch taller.

Anyway, for Sasquatch Days, Lynn's mom made her a blue and white polka-dot halter top. And she was going to wear it with jeans and her sandals.

Susan wanted some wedgies and I wanted a halter top, so we both saved up our money and went with Mama to the mainland when she went to get the groceries.

Susan found her wedgies right away. Black leather ones, with a strap and three little hearts cut out across the top. They were real pretty. Took all of her savings.

Then it was my turn, but I looked all over and I couldn't find a blue and white polka-dot halter top anywhere. Finally I found a blue and white halter top. But it was blue and white striped. Not polka-dot. And it wasn't even totally blue and white. It had a skinny red trim loop de looping all around the edges, the neck and waist and back. Another thing, it was too long. Almost to my hips, and Lynn's was short so you could see her bellybutton. I wanted one that showed my bellybutton. I have a nice bellybutton, nicer than hers. Hers sticks out a little bit.

But it was the only blue and white halter top I could find, and Mama was saying, "Come on, Anna, hurry it up. I want to catch the four o'clock ferry and we still have to drop the books off at the library!" So I bought it.

At least the price was right. On sale for a dollar ninety-nine.

When we got home I washed my jeans so the bum wouldn't be baggy, and found my pink zorries. They weren't quite sandals, but they were close enough. Then I took a bath. I asked Mama and got special permission as long as I gave Baby Will a bath after me. The water was nice and hot. I felt pretty luxurious. I washed my hair three times. Scrubbed and scrubbed with my fingers until my whole head hurt. Then I put some mayonnaise in my hair. Rubbed it in good before I rinsed.

Baby Will loved his bath. Anything to do with water

and he's happy. Taking a bath, playing in the creek, anything. He took a long bath. I made him lots of funny hairdos and showed him in the mirror and he laughed and laughed. So did I. He has this kind of gurgling glee when he laughs. It's like his whole chubby little body is laughing, even his toes. His face scrunches up so all you can see is this big grin, huge cheeks, and shining black button eyes. And you can't help but laugh too! Even if you're feeling sad.

After I got him off to bed, I stole Mama's razor out of the medicine cabinet and snuck it upstairs.

I shaved under my arms. I don't have any hair yet, but I heard that when you shave, it makes the hair grow faster. Then I snuck it back downstairs before Mama noticed it was gone. My underarms hurt.

The next morning there was excitement in the air. Like Christmas Eve or something. We lucked out on the weather too. It was perfect. Sunny and warm.

Sasquatch Days started at twelve-thirty. We wanted to be the first ones there, but Richard and Mama said no. We were leaving at three o'clock and that's that.

We left at four-fifteen.

I actually looked kind of pretty. I'd brushed my hair a hundred strokes. And it was all fluffy and shiny. Smelled a little bit like mayonnaise, but I just sprinkled some baby powder on my head and that made it smell nice.

The car ride over was pretty noisy.

When we got to Protected Point it was swarming! The whole island was there! Mama gave us each fifty cents and we split up.

I found Lynn at the concession stand. She was eating

a hot dog. Mustard and relish. It looked good, but I said I wasn't hungry. Hot dogs are too expensive.

She liked my halter top. Said it made me look like I had boobs. I looked, and she was right. All the stripes going around and around and then the way the fabric was kind of stretchy and had ridges running up and down, did make it look like I was starting to get boobs! Especially if I took a deep breath.

Lynn had some lip gloss, so after she finished her hot dog, we put it on. It was in a little pink heart-shaped container, had a mirror and everything. It smelled like perfume. Made our lips real slippery, and we pretended our lips were slipping right off our faces. It was funny.

There was a talent contest and a twenty-five-dollar prize. And they had a machine that would tell you who was the winner. Cause it would measure the applause. This tall skinny teenager won. He had long brown hair that kept falling in his eyes. He played the guitar and sang. Didn't sing very loud though. I sure wish I'd known they were having a talent contest. I would have won for sure. Could have sung something funny like "Kay was a little old man." Yeah, that would've been good. I would've sung it real loud. Like a professional. Worn overalls, cocked out my hip, put on an old straw hat maybe, and a piece of hay in my mouth. I would have been real funny. Made 'em laugh so hard their tummies would have hurt! I would have won for sure! Not only that, I sure could have made use of that twenty-five dollars! I mean that guy didn't even seem that happy to win. Didn't scream or anything. Just shuffled up, mumbled "Thanks" and shoved it in his pocket.

Lynn thought he was cute, but I didn't. I wish I had known. I could have won that contest for sure.

I went and bought myself a Fudgsicle with my money. Acted like it was no big deal. An everyday thing. Didn't even count my change. Lynn bought one too. And we sat on the bouncing ponies in the playground. The Fudgsicles were frozen really hard, our tongues got stuck on them. Ripped off a few taste buds. So we had to wait for a few minutes until they defrosted a bit, and then we ate them. They were good.

Katie and Julie tried to join us, but we ran away. Ran real fast, dodged in and out of people. Lost them. It was fun.

Found Susan and Lenny. They were sitting on the swings. Weren't swinging though. Just talking. We snuck up behind and made kissing noises and Susan chased us away.

We were still hungry so we went together on some french fries. Good ones, thick and greasy. We put lots of vinegar and catsup on them. They were really hot. And we had to tumble them around in our mouths before we could eat them.

It got darker. The band started to play. We kept eating, pretended like we didn't notice. Nervous. Didn't want to go, didn't want to stay. Ate our french fries, gently bouncing on the faded painted ponies. Feet making little dust puffs. Toes dirty.

Finally we were done. Threw the container in the garbage.

"How's my face?" said Lynn.

"Fine."

"No catsup?"

"No."

"You either."

We stood there for a minute and looked at each other. Then Lynn said, "You look pretty."

"You too," I said.

We remembered the lip gloss, so we put some on.

"You look pretty," she said again.

"You do too. Real pretty." We smiled at each other.

"Well . . ." she said.

"Well . . ." I said. And then we started over towards the dance floor. Not right to it, just over in that general direction. We ran into Peter and George. Peter has a big crush on Lynn, has ever since kindergarten.

"Hi," they said. "What cha doing?"

"Oh nothing . . ." we said, acting kind of bored. "Just kicking around."

"Pretty boring huh?"

"Yeah . . ." we said.

"You wanna go skip some rocks?"

We looked at each other, pretending to decide.

"I dunno . . ." said Lynn. "Do you wanna?"

I shrugged. "Might as well, there's nothing else to do."

They turned around and started walking towards the water. Walked way ahead of us. Heads leaned close together. They were talking but we couldn't hear cause it was too soft.

Lynn nudged me in the ribs.

"He's cute . . ." she whispered.

"Who is?"

"George!" she said, looking at me meaningfully. "He likes you!" I don't know why she said that cause he'd never looked at me twice.

"He does not!" I said.

"Yes he does!" She started laughing. I did too. I don't know why. Then she said, "I'm gonna kiss Peter." And I could tell she meant it.

It was kind of cold now that the sun had set. A bit of a breeze blowing off the ocean.

The boys started looking for rocks to skip. Normally I would have too. I'm a real good rock skipper. Once I jumped a rock fourteen times! It was a lucky fluke though. Cause normally I can only skip a rock four or five times, depending on the rock. It has to be good and flat. I prefer a slightly longish oval shape, better to wrap your fingers around. The secret to good rock skipping is finding the good rocks. And I'm good at that. I've got good eyes.

I like rock skipping, but somehow I didn't quite feel like it tonight.

Lynn and I sat down on a log and watched instead.

They weren't very good rock skippers. Didn't have the eye for the rock. They skipped for a long time.

It was cold on that log. I was shivering. So was Lynn. All of a sudden I felt mad, this was not my idea of a good time. I leaned over to Lynn.

"Let's go!" I said.

"No, wait a minute. They're almost done."

I knew she wanted to kiss Peter, so I waited. But they weren't almost done. They were nowhere near done. They just kept on skipping rocks and totally ignoring us. Us sitting on a log getting cold.

"Well I don't know about you," I said, "but I'm cold, I'm going!"

"No wait. Wait for just a minute."

"No!" I said grouchily. "This is no fun!" I stood up.

"We're going!" yelled Lynn.

The guys stopped skipping rocks right quick and scampered over. "Hey," they said, "why are you going?"

"Anna is cold."

"Oh . . ." said George. "Here, have my jacket." Just like that. "Have my jacket."

I said "No . . . no it's okay." But he took it off, even though he was only wearing a T-shirt underneath, and put it over my shoulders. It was a black jean jacket. Still warm from his body. Lynn smiled at me, and I could see that she and Peter were holding hands. She looked happy.

"We're gonna go for a walk," she said. "Wanna come?" I thought, how's she gonna kiss Peter if I'm with her, so I said, "Nah, I feel like sitting."

"But I don't want to leave you by yourself." she said.

And the next thing I knew, I heard George saying, "I'll stay."

"You don't have to," I said, feeling embarrassed. "I don't mind being by myself."

"No really, I'd like to." Just like that. "I'd like to." Like he really wanted to. Wasn't a chore or anything.

Once Lynn and Peter left I couldn't think of anything to say. Didn't know what to do with my arms and legs. Didn't know whether to sit or stand. He was looking at me. I could feel him looking at me. Me with his jean jacket around my shoulders.

"Wanna sit down?" he said.

"Sure," I said. I sat back down on the log.

He flopped on the ground beside me, his back against the log.

"Mmmm . . ." he said. "These pebbles are still warm." I leaned down and felt them.

"Ummm . . ." I said.

"Why don't you come down here?" He patted the pebbles with his hand. "It's out of the wind. Not so cold."

"Okay . . ." I said, acting casual. I got up and sat down beside him.

It was real dark now, and you could tell the dancing was getting real wild. Stomping, clapping, drunken fighting. But it all seemed far off, faint, like the bleed-through from another radio station.

"You're cold," he said. "You're still shivering."

Then he put his arm around me. We sat there. Just sat there and looked at the stars. They weren't hazy or blurry like sometimes they can get. They were real bright and clear. Clean. Just sat there and listened. Listened to the ocean. In and out, in and out. Continuous, constant.

Then almost as if in slow motion, our heads started moving towards each other. Slowly, slowly, almost not breathing. Closer, closer until our cheeks were almost touching. Close, so close I could feel the warmth of his cheek. The music playing, a seagull crying. We started to move again, slowly, slowly, turning our heads now, closer, closer, his breath on my face, mine on his, mingled breath, warm fragrant, closer, closer. Our lips almost touching. I was shivering, but my body was warm, warm all over. Like I'd been poured full of warm honey. Closer, closer, and then, his lips touched mine gentle, gentle, like they were barely there, softly, so softly, his lips touched mine. Rough, chapped and yet so gentle.

We didn't kiss again. Just sat there, didn't say a word. Happy, so happy. His arm holding me close like I was real special.

The next day I went back to Sasquatch Days, but he wasn't there. I hung around the dance floor, but he never showed up.

The Gordons showed up though. Richard and Betty Lou disappeared somewhere. And Mama and Mr. Gordon danced. They danced and danced and danced. Mama leaning in close. Breasts flopping, arms flailing, bodies rubbing, bumping. Eyes glittering, laughing, loud. Real loud.

I got bad asthma and Mama had to drive me home. I'd never had asthma before, so I was kind of scared. I didn't want Mama to go back. But she did. Gave me an asthma sprayer in case it got worse. Tucked me in bed, kissed me, and went back. Back to her dancing. Dancing with Mr. Gordon.

When I woke up, Susan was standing in the room, swaying a little.

"Susan?" I said. I felt funny, a little scared.

"Oh sorry . . . did I wake you?" It sounded like Susan, and looked like Susan, but I don't know, it just didn't feel like Susan. She started towards the bed and then I got real scared, cause all of a sudden I knew! It wasn't Susan. It was just someone pretending to be Susan! Someone pretending to be Susan so they could get in my bed. But it didn't trick me. I knew. I knew there was something different. Something in the eyes, and I wouldn't let her get in. Made her sleep in another room. Didn't fool me.

Community Dance

I had a call at the neighbors' house. It was Lynn and she was real excited. Peter had called her. Called her on the phone. Wanted to know if we wanted to go to the Foxfire Dance at the community hall! If we wanted to meet him and George there!

We were in heaven! A date! A real live date! A double date just like in the books!

My sisters were jealous. "It's not fair!" said Susan. "I'm the oldest!" And she stomped into her room. But then five minutes later out she came. Offered to help me curl my hair. Lent me the money for admission. Helped me choose what to wear.

I tried on a million tops, but none of them were right. "No," said Susan, shaking her head. "No, that doesn't seem quite right . . ." Then all of a sudden she jumped off the bed. *"I've got it!"* she yelled, and she ran out of the room. A second later she returned holding one of her favorite sweaters in her hand. The black one with little embroidered flowers scattered across the top. "Here!" she said, putting it in my hands. "Here, try it on!"

"Oh no!" I said, giving it back. "I couldn't!"

"Go ahead! Go ahead! Try it!" I tried it on and it looked beautiful. "Turn around," said Susan. So I turned around, this way and that. Both of us looking at me in the mirror. Me looking mysterious and grown up. We had so much fun, she even laughed a little. But then when Lynn and her mom came by to pick me up, Susan got all silent again. Got all silent and went in her room and shut the door.

We had Lynn's mom drop us off at the post office. Didn't want to seem like babies with her mom driving us and all. Lynn was wearing her halter top again. Said it was her good-luck top. She had curled her hair too, but it was already starting to fall. Her hair is so fine, it can never hold a curl for more than an hour or two. She took out her lip gloss and we put some on. Didn't talk much. We both were nervous I think. We walked over to the community hall. Could hear the rock and roll exploding out of the windows and doors. We had to pay two dollars and fifty cents each. The lights were dim. It was darker in the hall than outside. Had to squint to see.

"Do you see them?"

"Nope . . . do you?"

"No." She kicked her heel against the back of the door. "Jerks!"

"Let's look outside. Maybe they're outside . . ." We stuffed our hands in our jean pockets and went outside. Tried not to look anxious. Sauntered casually around the building. No guys.

"Fuck!" yelled Lynn. "Fuck! Fuck! Fuck!"

"Should we go? Do you want to go?" She flopped down on a big boulder. "Naah . . . Let's just wait for a while. They'll show up."

We waited. We waited an hour and a half, and finally they showed up. They were drunk. Very, very, very drunk.

It wasn't one little bit romantic. They could barely stand up. Had to lean on each other, careening from side to side like they were on the ferry in real rough water.

"Hi, Anna," said George, putting his face real close to mine, stupid grin on his face, eyes bugging out. "Hi, Anna, how are you today?" Then he and Peter started giggling like he just said the funniest thing in the world.

"You guys, stop being stupid." Lynn giggled.

"You guys," mimicked Peter, going all limp-wristed, "stop being stuuupid!" And then they fell on the ground shrieking with laughter. Lynn stopped giggling at me right quick. Grabbed a tight hold on the shoulder strap of her purse, swung it over her head and walloped him hard on the head. Walloped him a couple of times, gave George a whack too, stuck out her bottom lip and blew her corn-bleached hair out of her face and said, "Fuck you losers, eat my shit!" Then she put her purse back on her shoulders and marched away.

"Yeah! Fuck you!" I said, and scampered after her.

She was mad. Real mad. Never seen her quite that angry before. I didn't say anything, just half walked half ran beside her.

Finally she slowed down. "Losers . . . fucking losers . . . I can hardly wait until I'm grown up. Get off this fucking island."

"Where are you gonna go?"

"I don't know. Anywhere. Anywhere but here!" We walked along in silence for a while.

"Hey," she said, "want some fries? My treat."

We went by Mary's cafe. The fries were great. Lynn splurged and we got gravy on them. They were comforting. After we ate them Lynn looked at me out of the side of her eyes. "Let's not tell anybody about our date, okay?" I was glad she said that, cause I was going to ask her the same thing.

"It was pretty funny when you belted him on the head!"

"Yeah! Did you see his face? He didn't know what hit him!"

"Yeah!" I said happily. And we began laughing. Laughing and laughing, until the other customers started giving us dirty looks. "Oh fuck it!" I said in a loud voice. "Let's get out of this snotty place." So we left. Walked around the bay for a while. It was a real beautiful night. Dark clouds holding on to, and then releasing the moon. Lynn taught me the words to "Delta Dawn." It's a real pretty song. Kind of sad though.

When it got late enough, we called Lynn's mom and she picked us up.

"Have a good time at the dance?"

"Oh yeah, great!"

"Yeah, really great!"

"Best time ever!"

"Yeah, the *best!*" And we looked at each other and smiled.

Burnt Oatmeal

It was night. Lying in bed I could hear Mama and Richard in their bedroom arguing again. Him yelling, her voice cool cold precise. Him yelling. Louder and louder. Her quiet . . . calm. Then Richard started crying. Loud, noisy, gut-wrenching sobs. My body tense, cold under the blankets. I crawled out of bed, took my blanket with me. Wrapped it around my shoulders. The floor cold under my bare feet. Quietly, quietly I tiptoed out to the landing. Katie was already there, tears sliding silently down her face. I wrapped my blanket around her and we sat there, crouched at the top of the stairs listening. Listening to Richard sobbing and Mama being quiet.

When I woke, Mama was in the kitchen making breakfast. Which was very strange, cause I think the last time I saw her make anything was when I was five. It was oatmeal, and she burnt it.

I stood in the doorway and watched her. I watched Mama in her pajamas wander around, vague, lost, opening the wrong cupboards, trying to pretend she knew what she was doing, where things were.

"Want some help, Mama?" I asked. She jumped. "What?" she asked, almost guilty. "Do you want some help?" I repeated patiently. She breathed, relieved. I don't know why.

"Help," she said. Then "Yes . . . Yes, that would be nice." I came in. "What are you making?"

"Cereal . . . dry cereal."

"It's here," I said. I took it out of the cupboard and plopped it on the table. I don't know why, but all of a sudden I felt angry. Real angry. I grabbed the pitcher of milk and slammed it on the table. Slopping out trembling angry puddles! Sugar bowl! Bang! Then the spoons, the bowls, cups! Banging each thing down, down on the table, naming it as I did. Bang! "Milk!" Bang! "Sugar!" Bang! "Bowls!" Shouting now . . . *Bang! "Spoons!" Bang! "Cups!"* . . . I stood there for a moment breathing hard. Not looking at her standing hurt, helpless, lost, in the center of the kitchen. Then I stomped past her, bumping her arm, pretending it was an accident. I ran up the stairs and screamed, "Breakfast is ready!" Stood in the hall and screamed it till my face was purple.

When I came back in, Mama was sitting at the table. Still . . . empty . . . fragile. I stood there uncertain, anger gone, listening to the both of us, hearts pounding, breathing.

Then Mama spoke. Quietly, without moving. So quietly I could hardly hear her . . . but it didn't matter, cause my tummy already knew what she was going to say.

"Richard's gone," she whispered.

"I know," I said.

Baby Will

Richard came back home. He was lonely I guess after being away from all us kids.

I was feeding the chickens when I heard Joy shout. "Daddy's comin', Daddy's comin' back!" I dropped the bag of chicken feed and ran, ran to the front of the house. The rest of the kids, already there, standing silent. Squinting against the bright sunlight and dust. Bodies empty, like all the sand had been poured through. Empty, waiting.

The rusty red Volkswagen bug roared up the drive and lurched to a stop. Clouds of dust billowing, stinging our eyes almost like crying. He staggered out, slammed his door, eyes staring at us, through us, frozen invisible.

Then we heard the front door open. He heard it too. He swiveled and stared, stared over our heads. And it comes out, comes out of his gut like a bad taste, "You . . . cunt . . . You fucking *cunt!*" Building like a volcano. *"You fucking goddamn fucking cunt!"* Mama doesn't answer. Just stands there still, arms crossed, gripping tightly. *"You cunt!"* He screams and then grabs a handful of dirt and another and another and throws them at her. Little bits of stone and twigs hit her and fall, but most of it just makes little dust puffs in the air, tears going down his face. *"You cunt you fucking cunt."* Then he runs back to the car and pulls out the thirty-odd-six and points it at her. She doesn't move, she just looks at him right in the eyes. And he looks at her.

It was kind of a weird look actually, not like he was pointing a gun at her or anything. It was real open, vulnerable, almost tender, like they were gonna kiss or something. Then all of a sudden he screamed, *"Don't anybody move!"* Not that any of us were planning on it. I mean what did he think we were, crazy?

Then he started doing this weird sort of sidestep, waving the gun back and forth between Mama and us kids. Sidestepping closer to us kids, closer, closer. "Don't anybody *move! Don't anybody move!"* Then suddenly he reached over and grabbed Baby Will around the waist. "Stay where you are or I'll kill him!" he yelled. So none of us moved. We didn't want Baby Will to be dead. We didn't want to be dead either, so we just stood there and watched Richard run back to the car, throw the gun in the back seat and drive off with Will on his lap. Will crying cause he'd dropped his yellow Tonka truck.

Disengaging

When we came home from school Mama was already there. On the phone again.

Lately Mama was always on the phone. In the morning she'd get up early before the rest of the family, with her maps, charts, felt pens and lists. Phoning telephone operators. Talking, crying, begging for information, any information, new listings, unlisted numbers . . . Any new phone numbers perhaps, any new unlisted ones? Talking, talking . . . Sometimes casual, offhand, "an old friend," or "a family member has died, a will, must get in touch . . ." or a distorted version of the truth, tears, "my baby, stolen, kidnapped . . ." crying, long conversations. Long conversations with telephone operators. Marking down, crossing off, making charts, more charts, new charts until it was time for her to go to school and teach. Then when we'd get home there she'd be again. Hunched over the phone.

So as I was saying, Mama was on the phone again. Crying this time, crying and blowing her nose. Joy and I went outside and took turns on the swing. It was a rope swing, on this big old tree, oak or maple or something. It had big thick gnarled branches and wide cool leaves. The rope was tied around this huge branch that hung out over the cliff. A big cliff! At least an eight- or nine-foot drop! Tied tight so it wouldn't come off, with a large knot at the bottom which you could either hold on to, which was quite difficult on your shoulder and arm muscles, or you could sit on it, wrapping your legs tight around each other, pulling your body in close, clinging to the thick rough rope. I preferred to sit, because as I pointed out, the swing is over a cliff, and so it wouldn't feel too good if you fell. Either way, sitting or hanging, your belly lurched when you pushed off.

So we were swinging, whooping it up, having a good time, when Mama came outside. It was Joy's turn, and she was swinging around. Holding on with her arms, pumping her legs, head thrown back, sunshine on her face, big happy freckled smile.

"Joy," said Mama. Joy didn't answer cause she was swinging and the wind was in her ears. "Joy," yelled Mama. "Yeah, Mama!" yelled Joy. Toffee hair whipping around her face. "Joy! Get down! I have something to tell you."

She scrambled down and stood before Mama, panting a little from the swing, a Band-Aid half peeled off her knee, the dark crusty scab underneath. Orange shorts, dusty, pulled up kind of lopsided, head cocked to one side, expectant, like a puppy, an overgrown eager puppy.

Joy and Mama. It was funny really, now that I think about it, cause Mama seemed unfamiliar. I'd known her all my life, but there she stood, and I didn't even recognize her. I guess because I'd never seen her by the swing before, maybe that was it. Anyway, they stood there looking at each other and then Mama said, "Joy, you're going to go visit your mother. Your real mother. I've written to her and she'd like for you to come for a visit." Joy didn't say anything. She just looked at Mama like she'd been hit over the head, so Mama continued. "She hasn't seen you in six years, almost seven. She would like to, so you are going. You are going to visit your mother, your real mother . . ." "Is Anna coming or Katie?" asked Joy in a small voice. "No, but Faith will be there." "Or Susan . . . or—" "No!" Mama said, cutting her off. "Just you. She's your mother. Your real mother . . . And she wants you to come." "Mama," said Joy in a tiny tiny voice. "I don't want to go." Mama continued louder in all that stillness, pretending not to hear. "And she wants you to come for a visit." I could see Joy shaking, trembling all over. Then she flung herself on Mama, eyes huge dark lost, her voice coming out in big sobs. "Don't make me go, Mama! Please don't make me go away!" But it didn't help, only made Mama grouchier. "Don't be so melodramatic, Joy," she said irritably, words clipped. "It's no great tragedy to visit your mother." "She's not my mother. You're my mother, Mama! You're my mother! I love you!" It came bursting out of Joy. Exploding, overflowing passion. "You! I don't even know what she looks like! Don't make me go . . . please don't make me go . . ."

But Mama stood rigid. Arms held out to her sides so she wouldn't get any cooties. Face like she's smelling a bad smell.

Finally Joy ran out of words and just sobbed over and over again, "I love *you* Mama . . . I love *you* . . ."

But Mama disengaged herself and went back inside the house and shut the door. Shut the door to make some more phone calls. More phone calls to telephone operators. Phone calls and charts.

Good Times

Sam's dad bought him a bottle of cherry liqueur.

Me and Lynn drank it with him and Peter behind the gym. The whole thing. Me and Lynn drank the most. It tasted good. We sure got drunk. Good and drunk.

The guys tried to cop a feel. I think it was kind of disappointing for them though, cause neither Lynn nor I have any breasts whatsoever. They might just as well have stuck their hands up each other's shirts for all the difference there was. Oh well, they seemed to want to, so who cares.

When they'd finished groping around for our nonexistent breasts, Lynn and I decided we were going to crash the seventh graders' dance. So we got up and headed for the gym. It was real funny trying to walk, the world kept tipping. Lynn walked right into a tree. So hard that it knocked her over. It was funny. We laughed so hard that I had to pee. Couldn't hold it. Pulled my pants down and peed right there on the ground. Didn't even care.

Then I helped Lynn up and somehow or another we got to the gym.

They wouldn't let us in. They said we were too young. Someone noticed we were drunk. And everyone crowded around and started laughing at us. I guess they figured we were too young to drink too. I don't like being laughed at or condescended to, I don't care how big they are. So I punched a few people. I don't quite remember who. But they just kept laughing, so we left. We didn't want to go to their stupid dance anyway.

I got the cherry liqueur bottle and broke it on the side of the gym. Then Lynn threw up. I felt sick, but I didn't. I can hold my liquor.

Sam and Peter came back. They wanted to feel us down there. We told them to fuck off, and went home.

Ground Beef

Mama decided she was scared. Scared to stay in the house anymore. Scared that Richard would come and steal the rest of us. So we moved into Mr. Gordon's trailer in town. He let us stay there because it was safer, not so isolated. And Mr. Gordon moved into the logger's camp. He was a logger, most of the men on the island were. Loggers, miners, and layabouts, those were basically your three categories. There was one artist, Frank Gilpin, and one writer, Colin McLean. So anyway, Mr. Gordon let us use his trailer and he moved into the camp down the road. He wasn't living with Betty Lou anymore.

Last week he went by his old house to see his boys, and Betty Lou chased him around the front yard with an ax! Lynn was riding by on her bike, and she knew he was dating my mom, so she called me up on the phone and told me. She said it was real funny. Her so tiny and him so big. Her chasing him around in her bathrobe, waving the ax in big circles over her head, screaming at the top of her lungs. That I would have liked to have seen. Probably better that I didn't though, as I would have died laughing. Actually, I probably would have died of death, cause he would have killed me for sure. He doesn't have much of a sense of humor.

Anyway I was in the kitchen making some spaghetti. It was kind of difficult, cause the kitchen in that trailer is real small and cramped, and I didn't have all my spices and things. But I didn't complain. Pretended it was real nice, like a little toy house or something. Anyway, I needed some more hamburger. So Mama asked Mr. Gordon nice and flirty if he perhaps could go and get some. Well he did. Brought it back, made a real big deal out of it, like it was a roast beef or something. When all it was, was one lousy pound of cheap fatty ground beef. Anyway, I took it. And cooked it. And we ate it, even him.

Well, that night, I woke up cause he was yelling. I was the only one who woke up cause I was in the bedroom closest to the living room.

There were two bedrooms in his trailer. One in front, which I shared with Mama. I slept on the floor and she slept on the bed. I got to sleep with Mama cause I was quiet. And Katie and Susan slept in the bedroom in the back, cause they were noisy and messy. It was a privilege to share a bedroom with Mama, but I kind of wished I was with my sisters. Maybe then Susan would start talking to me again, the way she used to.

The trailer was small, but we rattled around in it. Big

gaping holes gouged out of the family. Not even a family really, just the fractured splinters of a glass after it has been hurled against a wall. We were the pieces. Just little broken pieces of glass.

Anyway, Mr. Gordon was yelling and I woke up. But Susan and Katie were in the back, so they didn't. They didn't hear. Didn't hear him yelling and swearing. Swearing about us. That he'd bought us meat! Bought us meat! Put food in our mouths! But did we say thank you? Were we grateful? No! No, we were spoiled rotten little snot-nosed kids! Well he'd had it! Had it up to here! Was gonna chop us up! Chop us up with that ax he'd taken from Betty Lou. Make the world a better place!

But the scariest thing was, Mama wasn't screaming or crying. She was laughing. Fits of laughter. Like what he was talking about was funny. Real funny. Laughing and laughing and laughing.

Had to save my family. Had to save them.

I got up and ran to the window several times before my body actually got up. It was like I was moving under a sea of molasses. A thick black heavy sea of molasses.

I got the screen off. Wound open the window as far as it could go. Good thing I was skinny or I never would have been able to squeeze out of that window. I ran. Ran in my nightgown through the bushes to the next-door neighbors' house. The Toporowskis.

I knocked on the door. No answer. I knocked harder. Harder. Two fists.

Footsteps. The door opened. Mr. Toporowski looked out. He was wearing pajama bottoms, putting on his glasses. Sleepy squished face, hair standing up.

"Yes . . . May I help you?" Mrs. Toporowski was

standing behind him. Peering over his shoulder, putting on her bathrobe.

I started to cry. Trying to act like I wasn't, trying to be polite.

"Please, sir . . . Could you help me please . . . Mr. Gordon is going to chop up my family with an ax."

"Wha . . . wha . . . what's this?" he said, looking confused.

"Mr. Gordon, he's gonna chop up my family with an ax! Please come now . . . please help me . . . please stop him."

I could see Rhonda poking her head out of her bedroom. She was in my grade. It made me uncomfortable, cause I was supposed to be cool and she was supposed to be the geek that nobody wanted to play with. And yet here I was crying on her doorstep. Crying on her doorstep and begging for help.

"You better go, Frankie," said Mrs. Toporowski. "Go check it out."

"All right," he said. I could tell he was scared. He wasn't very big. "I'll go see what's going on."

She helped him put on his coat and we started back through the bushes.

When we got close he put his hand on my arm. "Where is he?" he whispered.

"In the living room, right over there."

I pointed.

"Stay here," he said. Then he went over, crouched down outside the window and listened.

I couldn't hear what they were saying from where I was, but I could tell he was getting worried. I could tell he believed me now.

He came back.

"Okay . . ." he said. "Okay . . . well . . . I guess we better . . ." He cleared his throat. "Okay . . ." he said. "I guess I better . . . we better . . . Ahem . . . I sure wish we had police on this island . . . oh well . . . Okay." He took a breath. "Come on."

We walked up to the trailer door. Him in front.

He took another breath and knocked.

"What's that!" said Mr. Gordon.

"Just the door," said Mama. "My you're jumpy."

When she opened the door she was smiling.

"Yes," she said. "Can I help you." Smiling. Smiling brightly until she saw me. Me behind Mr. Toporowski.

"Uhh . . ." said Mr. Toporowski. "Uhh . . . What seems to be the trouble here?"

"Trouble? There's no trouble here," said Mama, smiling again, eyes like steel. "Come here, Anna. What are you doing out there in your nightgown? Come inside, you're gonna catch your death of a cold."

I didn't go in. Stayed behind Mr. Toporowski.

"So there's no trouble here? Everything's okay?" He paused. Looking uncomfortable. "Umm . . . Horton?" Mr. Toporowski said, poking his head in the room. "Horton? . . . Are you okay?"

Mr. Gordon didn't answer right away, just looked at his hands between his knees. His big old hands with one finger missing. One finger missing that he'd lost in the war.

"Horton?" said Mr. Toporowski again.

"Yeah . . ." Mr. Gordon said. "Yeah, I'm okay . . ."

Mr. Toporowski looked at me.

"Are you okay?" he asked.

Mama grabbed my arm. Gripped it tight. "She's fine,"

she said, squeezing it hard. Smiling, still smiling at Mr. Toporowski. "She just had a bad dream. Didn't you, Anna?" She shook my arm to make me answer, but I couldn't. "She just had a bad dream, that's all." And she pulled me inside and shut the door.

As the door was shutting I could see Mr. Toporowski. Shifting from foot to foot, wondering what to do.

Mama took me inside. Put me in bed. Didn't talk to me. Ice cold, and yet, it was just a bad dream so she couldn't say anything. Put me in bed and went out to the living room. Out to the living room to talk in a low voice with Mr. Gordon.

In the morning she moved me to my sisters' room. Said I made too much noise. Kept her up at night.

Sandra's

I got invited over to Sandra Walker's house for a sleepover. So I went.

Lynn was real mad. Said Sandra was a big fat cow. And boring too. Said she hoped I fell over dead of boredom.

Mama wasn't happy either. She feels the Walkers are common, and I shouldn't associate with them.

But I went anyway.

And Lynn was right. Sandra was boring. I mean it's funny, we did real exciting things. Borrowed her grandma's nail polish and painted our fingernails blood red. Made chili con carne. Stayed up late.

But it was boring. The only exciting thing was when her grandma went over to the mainland to the pub and came back on the last ferry rip-roaring drunk. And Sandra's dad had to go and pick her up cause she was causing a public disturbance.

He brought her back with her fake fur, orange-dyed hair, and red, red nails. Her makeup was all smeared, and she was shrieking out the worst kind of swear words that most grown-ups pretend they don't know.

But Sandra's family was just so matter-of-fact. Peeled her out of her skintight clothes, washed her face, and put her to bed. No big deal. And actually it wasn't, cause Sandra told me later, rather apologetically, that her grandma got drunk most Fridays and Saturdays, and you just kind of had to get used to it.

So even this wasn't so exciting. But you know, I kind of liked it. Everything so placid and slow. Everything so boring.

It was kind of nice.

So I think next time Sandra asks me, I'll sleep over again.

Gang Bang

I must have slept in, cause when I woke up, Katie and Susan were already gone. Their blankets rumpled and empty. Gray light choking through the dust-clotted screens on the wind-shut windows.

It must be cloudy.

Slid off the bunk bed. Toes recoiling as they hit the floor. I always thought I wanted carpet, but the carpet in Mr. Gordon's trailer was scudzey. It smelled of stale beer and cigarette butts. And it's so short, it's almost not like carpet at all. Rough too. When I grow up I'm going to have carpets in every room. Real carpets. Deep and plush carpet, like moss in the forest. And shag carpet too. Lynn has shag carpet at her house. Lots of it. Gold shag.

I heard Mama murmuring in the living room. Nobody was answering, so she must be on the phone again.

I got dressed quickly. Wanted to get out before she got off the phone. Didn't want to face her needy eyes.

Wiggled into my jean shorts. I must be growing again, cause they're getting tight. I had to lie on the floor to button the fly. Then I put on my halter top. The one that makes me look like I have boobs. There was a little splat of gravy from last night's beef stew, but I scraped it with my thumbnail and used a bit of spit and it looked okay.

I took a breath at the bedroom door and opened it. Mama looked up. I walked by, almost like I didn't even see her. Her and her charts. Walked fast so she'd know I'm in a hurry. I went to the fridge. Not much there. Mama was hanging up the phone, had to move fast.

I plunged my hand in the pickle jar, felt around, grabbed a big one, slapped on the lid and slammed the fridge shut with my foot.

"Anna," said Mama.

"Gotta go, Mama, I'm late."

My hand was dripping pickle juice on Mr. Gordon's floor, so I shook it off in the sink.

I knew she wanted to talk, so I spoke before she could.

"Something's wrong with the fridge. There's ice on the pickles."

"Oh dear . . ."

"Not too bad though, just a thin layer."

I slipped on my zorries and out the door I went. Quickly before she could speak.

I didn't look back, cause I knew she'd be sitting there, gagged and bound, watching me escape.

There is only one way to eat a pickle that's satisfying. First you stick the whole thing in your mouth, doesn't matter how big it is. Then slurp, suck off the juice as you slide it out of your mouth. This you repeat three or four times until all the outside juice is gone. Then nibble off the end, and suck the juice and seeds out of the middle. Then crunch, crunch, crunch . . . *gobble it up!* And that's the way I ate it.

It was good. I wished Mama wasn't home, otherwise I would have gone straight back home, lickity split, and got myself another one. Would have got myself a sweater too. It was kind of cold.

I went down to Mary's cafe. It was nice and warm.

Mary poked her hairnetted head out of the kitchen.

"Can I help you?" she rasped in her tired-out voice.

"Just looking," I said, pretending to try and decide if I wanted to buy a candy bar or something. But she didn't go back into the kitchen. Just stood there watching me. And since I didn't have any money I left. I think she thought I wanted to steal something.

My hand smelled like pickle juice, so I washed it off in the bay. I myself don't mind the smell of pickle juice, but you never know who you might meet, or how they might respond to pickle smell.

I walked by the elementary school. No one there. I swung on the swings for a while, but it's kind of boring to swing by yourself, so I left.

Peter, Sam and George were hanging out behind John's hardware.

I pretended not to see them.

"Hey, Anna," they yelled.

I turned around real casual like.

"Oh hi," I said like I'd just noticed them. "What are you guys doing?"

"Gonna smoke a joint," said Peter. "Wanna join us?"

"Okay," I said, feeling like a traitor, cause actually Peter is Lynn's boyfriend. "Why not, I don't have anything better to do."

"Well," said George. "We'd better not smoke it here, we might get busted."

"Yeah," said Peter. "Don't wanna get busted."

So we headed out the old back road. The three guys loping on ahead. Me ambling behind. Hands stuffed in my front pockets. Wanting to back out, but already committed.

A slight mist was starting to fall. Kissing my legs, arms, eyelashes.

We were pretty far in the woods when they finally stopped.

I wished Lynn was with me.

Peter lit up.

It took two matches.

He took the first toke. Then he handed it to Sam.

Sam took a hit and handed it to me.

It became real quiet. Real quiet. They all watched me concentrated like.

I was glad I'd smoked before. I took a long toke to show them I knew how. Held it deep, deep in my lungs. Scorching, searing, like Drano in my throat. Eyes watering. Wanting to cough, choke like I did with Lynn, but I didn't.

They passed the joint around and around. But somehow it seemed to get to me twice as often as everybody else. I guess cause I was the girl or something.

Everything was fine, just fine, standing around in the misting rain, smoking pot with the guys, and then all of a sudden I was stoned. Real stoned. I'd thought I'd gotten stoned with Sandra and Lynn, but I guess I hadn't. Cause it was nothing like this. Their faces swooping in and out. The trees stretching up into forever, leaning on me, weighing on me, suffocating me so I couldn't breathe.

"Water . . ." I mumbled. "I need some water." And I backed away.

"Hey, Anna! Where are you going?" one of them yelled.

"Water," I said, trying to act normal. "I need some water."

I went crashing through the woods until I found a

creek. I kneeled down and drank and drank and drank. I could hear them laughing up on the bank. Laughing and laughing. "Look at her! Drinking like an animal!" "Ha ha ha." "Boy did we ever get her stoned!"

Ha ha ha real funny. I got up and wiped off my mouth with the back of my arm.

It was raining harder now.

My legs were scratched up by the brambles, crimson droplets of blood mixed with rain and mud.

"Hey, Anna!" yelled Peter. "Hey, Anna! Wanna gang bang?"

I didn't know what that was, but I was scared.

"Fuck off!" I yelled and started to walk away.

They followed me, laughing.

"Hey, Anna. How about a gang bang, huh? I bet you'd like it."

"Fuck off!" I screamed and I started to run. I started to run fast, and they chased me.

They aren't laughing now. Faster and faster I run. I run and I run and I run. Heart pounding, rain beating down. Gotta get to the lake, gotta get to the lake, so I can hide in the tall grasses.

I get there. Run into the grasses, get down on my hands and knees. Crawl quickly, quietly.

They get there.

"She can't have gone far!"

"Spread out!"

I hear them looking. Looking for me. Beating the grasses with a stick.

And I crouch into a little tiny ball. Try to stop my shaking. Mouth bitter and dry.

They look for a long time.

Finally Sam says, "Oh come on, let's go." He sounds kind of embarrassed.

"No," says Peter. "We're gonna find the bitch."

"Well," says Sam, "I don't know about you, but I'm going." And I hear him leave.

Peter and George look for me a little bit longer, and then they leave too.

But I don't come out. I stay there all curled up. Shaking and crying, until it gets dark, then I creep back to the trailer.

Lynn and Sandra

Lynn doesn't believe me about Peter and George and Sam. Says I'm just making it up.

Her cheeks got real red when I told her. I thought she was going to slap me. Said I was just trying to break her and Peter up cause I was jealous.

And now she's best friends with Sandra. Won't even talk to me. Just tosses her long blond hair and looks the other way.

They won't eat lunch with me or anything.

As a matter of fact, no one will. The only person who offered was Rhonda Toporowski, and I said no. Cause I knew she was feeling sorry for me. And if there is one thing I can't stand, it's being pitied.

So now I sit on the top of the jungle gym, eat my lunch by myself, and pretend I like it.

Defrosting

It was cold. Everything was frozen over. The lakes, the rivers, the pumps, the pipes. The roads froze over, with black ice, and Ron the school bus driver told us kids that we had to "keep it down," cause the roads were real dangerous, and he had to concentrate or we'd all crash and be dead.

Even the bay was starting to freeze over! That's how cold it was. As far back as everybody could remember the bay had never frozen over, cause the bay was salt water. And it is very difficult for salt water to freeze. Very difficult.

So we were on the bus, Lynn and Sandra sitting together. Sitting together talking in hushed tones about how frozen over everything was. Me sitting there listening, pretending I wasn't. Then Sam said he'd read in the newspaper that there was this club. This club called the Polar Bear Club. And every New Year's Day, they all go for a swim in the bay. Then he laughed and said he bet they were going to pass this year. And Lynn laughed and said, "Yeah, nobody could get in the water this year!" "Yeah!" said Sandra. "You'd have to be crazy!" But I could see that underneath all their talk they were impressed by people who could do this. Amazed.

So I said, "I don't think it's such a big deal."

Nobody really paid any attention, so I said it again. Louder. "I don't think it's such a big deal to swim in the bay!"

Well if the bus was quiet before, it became even quieter now. Everybody just stopped talking and looked at me.

"Yeah," I said loudly. "No big deal. As a matter of fact, I think I'll take a little dip today!"

Everyone started laughing, talking, shouting! Ron the bus driver kept yelling, "Quieten down! Shut up!" But it didn't do any good. Everybody kept screaming and hollering at the top of their lungs. They seemed to think it was a big joke. That I'd never do it. I was kind of scared myself.

The bus stopped at Protected Point.

When I got out, so did half the bus, teasing, jeering, pushing, laughing. I was excited. Scared. I took off my coat and gave it to Katie. She was pulling on my arm crying, "Don't do it, Anna . . . don't do it." Then I took off my snow boots and slipped out of my jeans. Lucky thing I was wearing a bodysuit. A red bodysuit. Turtleneck.

"Come on, Anna," whispered Susan, smoothing down my hair. "Let's go home, come on, honey."

"No," I said, my face hot. "No. I feel like a swim."

Off came my socks and hat. Just my bodysuit left. Nothing left to do, nothing left to take off. So I marched barefoot in the snow to the bay. As I walked away from the crowd, I heard it grow quiet. I could feel them watching. Watching me. Me! I could feel their excitement.

When I got to the water I didn't stop. Didn't break my pace. Didn't make a noise. Ice, breaking, cutting. Water so cold it burnt. Onward. Up to my waist, burning-hot numbness. Couldn't breathe. I was shaking, shaking uncontrollably. Still no noise. Too far away for them to hear. But still no noise, might lose it, lose control. I forced myself to take a breath. A big breath. Needed pressure, willpower to force my lungs open. A breath, I took a big squeezed breath, shut my eyes, and dove in. In under. Cold . . . cold . . . heart stopping, body panicking. I'm going to die. Arms flail, I surfaced, head pounding, body screaming, aching, searing. I did it! *I did it!* Arms shooting into the air, tight fists of victory! Faint cries, whistles, applause drifting in from the shore to my rushing ears.

I took another breath and plunged back in again . . . and again . . . and again, until I couldn't stand it any longer. Then I stood up and walked to the shore. Walked slowly, savoring every moment. I had done it. I had done the impossible.

I knew then at that moment that I could do anything. Anything in the world I set my mind to.

When I reached the shore, everyone crowded around me. Me the star! Pounding me on the back, congratulating me, wrapping their coats around me. Susan hugging me, rubbing me up and down to keep me warm. "You did it!" she whispered in my ear. "You did it!" Sandra and Lynn's excited envious faces pushing in. Even better when Katie screamed, "She's bleeding! Anna is bleeding!" Seems the ice had cut my legs. I didn't cry, even though there was a lot of blood. People thought it was because I was brave. But the fact of the matter was, my legs were too frozen and I couldn't feel a thing.

When I got home and defrosted, now that is another story.